CROATOAN

THE LIGHTHOUSE KIDS

Spirits of Cape Hatteras Island

CROATOAN

Jeanette Gray Finnegan Jr.

CONTENTS

Storm's a-Comin'

The wind was beginning to lift the swing higher and higher. Ellie pumped her legs as far out as she could, straining toward the air and hoping for the clouds.

"Look, Ellie, I'm almost as high as you are," Blake yelled, excitement filling his voice.

"My ropes are buckling. Look, look, look!" Her excitement matched that of her cousin, and she knew she had won. "Blake, let's quit. Here comes Luke. Grandpop must be coming."

"Look at me, Luke. I'm flying!" Blake was beginning to stretch his legs straight out, even pointing his shoeless toes.

"Blake, stop going so high. You're gonna fall off, and then what will happen? Grandpop is comin' up the hill, and we need to get outta here. Don't forget to get your shoes. I'm tired of looking for them!" Luke, who was always the one who herded everybody together, came toward them, and both younger children listened, stopped their swinging, picked up their shoes, and followed him. They did not mind doing what Luke asked, as they loved him more than anyone. Both wanted to be just like him. After all, he was always the one to get them out of their biggest scrapes. He was the oldest of the three and by far the most dependable.

The hurricane was coming. All the other children and adults had left the schoolhouse and gone home to prepare. School let out early, as those who lived in neighboring villages had to get home ahead of the coming storm. The school served all seven of the villages, from Rodanthe to Hatteras, and the used commando trucks that the navy gave to the island arrived ahead of time to make the trek through the mostly sandy roads to the farthest villages. Luke, Ellie, and Blake lived at the lighthouse, the tall structure situated on the beach about three miles east from the edge of Buxton, the village located in the island's center.

About thirty miles from the mainland and surrounded on all sides by water, Hatteras Island was made up of seven villages. The northernmost village of Rodanthe, south to Waves, and Salvo were collectively called Chicamacomico; then came Kinnakeet, Buxton, Trent, and finally Hatteras, the last village before the next island, Ocracoke. As Buxton was in the middle of the fifty-mile island, the school was built there.

When all the buses left, Ellie and Blake hit the swings in the schoolyard. They were both anxious to get to the rope swing first because it had the best seat, and usually during recess all three were occupied by the older kids. Sometimes the high school girls just sat there and talked, not even swinging. That was a waste of time, according to Ellie, who at the time had already reached her perch on the favored swing. Blake gave out an audible sigh as he was forced to take what was left. The middle one remained vacant in hopes that Luke would join them, because they both wanted to be beside him. They had been instructed to wait until Grandpop came to pick them up.

Aunt Nett, Luke and Blake's mom, who taught the first, second, and third grades (all in the same room) also stayed late because she had some work to do in order to secure the room in case the windows blew out or the roof leaked. This was a serious hurricane. Grandpop picked up word of it on the radio. It had already hit Cuba, so they knew the strength. Now it was heading up the Florida coast. She was packing winds of up to eighty-five miles per hour and picking up speed.

Grandpop had been consulting with the Coast Guard, and everyone was warned to begin preparations for the coming wind and rain. It was no small job to inform the island, as few places had telephones. Fortunately, Captain Charlie Gray, the children's grandfather, had one. As the head lightkeeper for the Cape Hatteras Lighthouse, his responsibility was to keep the beacon burning in order to warn the ships at sea. The other telephones were scattered throughout the island. The Coast Guard station had several, depending on each department's need. Others were placed at the general store in each village. Hatteras and Rodanthe had extra telephones in the government facilities located there: Hatteras had telephones at the Weather Bureau and the ferry docks, where ferries ran often to carry people and goods from Hatteras Island to Ocracoke Island. Rodanthe had a phone inside the lifesaving station in the middle of the village.

Most of the men on the island made their living from some type of fishing. Several fished offshore in locally built heavy boats made for battling the sea, catching large fish such as tuna, wahoo, mahi-mahi, and swordfish. Some others were seagoing shrimp boats, built to withstand the pitch and roll of the Atlantic's heavy seas. Still others made their living from the Pamlico Sound, using pound nets for catching schools of fish and crab pots scattered across the water, and collecting the bounty from oyster and clam beds they farmed in secret spots of their seeding. The men were on the water day after day, pulling in sea life to sell across the sound or to be consumed at home. This constant communication with nature allowed them to notice differences in the weather and the changes, no matter how slight, in the environment around them. Grandpop was always saying, "I smell a shift of wind," and within minutes the wind picked up speed, the horizon turned dark, and a fresh scent of air went across the land.

The smell of the atmosphere was so different that it was impossible to describe, but it always brought on a smile in the *knowing*. On the water, some fishermen could "see the sound swell," aware that the seas around them were about to change. The usually calm water began to turn dark blue, with small whitecaps forming at the tide tip of the movement of the swells. They were not choppy swells but a full, robust filling of the sound. There was always a push of water into the channel from the ocean when a storm was coming. As a result, the islanders really didn't need the telephone to alert them that a hurricane was coming. They already knew. The signs were there and in plenty of time to prepare.

Ellie lived with her grandparents. She was the granddaughter of Captain Charlie and his wife, Odessa. Captain Charlie was responsible for the care and maintenance of the mighty brick lighthouse located at the edge of the beach where the island jutted out farthest to sea. About two miles directly off the coast from the Cape Hatteras Light, a group of three enormous undersea mountains of shifting sand rose up, in places reaching from twenty feet to three and one half feet below the surface. None of the charts were dependable when it came to marking the water in that area. Because of this hazardous and unstable stretch of land hiding beneath the sea, ships took care to avoid the area altogether. This unseen danger was the scourge of ships attempting to travel from north to south, or vice versa. The only ships caught in this region of ocean were either uninformed or had been blown off course to flounder helplessly against the shoals. It truly was the "graveyard of the Atlantic." More than 600 shipwrecks had occurred there.

Ships used two waterways to move up the coast. One was the warm waters of the Gulf Stream, described as a river flowing in the middle of the Atlantic Ocean. The Gulf Stream even had a different color that was easily spotted: the deepest of blue, right beside the greenish blue of the ocean. Anglers have caught the largest blue marlin swordfish and sailfish in these waters, as they made their way up the warm stream and followed it around to the shores of Europe. The other waterway, known as the Labrador Current, was a cold-water current, coming down from the Arctic Ocean to meander along the northern coast of the United States. These two natural forces—one warm water, the other cold—collided at the landmass of sand marking the point of the island of Cape Hatteras. This meeting produced a heavy fog and a powerful clash of waves. Water usually sprayed up several stories high at the point of impact. Fishing at this spot was perilous and plentiful.

In the area, which locals called "The Point"—about one mile south of the lighthouse—fishing by the island's residents made for a bountiful harvest. The Point was occupied year round by anglers hoping to catch the "big one." While families fished The Point, children were only allowed to play on the beach, at a visible distance from the wash. The water, shifting and rough, caused even experienced anglers not to venture too far out. The best bet for catching fish in this tempestuous water was a strong casting arm to get the line far enough out into the water for the fish to bite. Most of the local men—and a few of the women—were experts at that. As the younger ones played near the area, their families fished the sandbar at low tide. The sandbar on occasion stuck out so far that the fish literally bumped into it, but all knew better than to step too far into the churning ocean, lest they be sucked out to sea. The Point was a grown-up thing. Youngsters were just lucky to tag along.

Grandpop's old jalopy came up the pine-covered road through the trees until it reached the clearing where the schoolhouse was located.

"Mom, come on. Grandpop's here! Let's go!" Luke shouted toward the swings, "Blake, come on! Grandpop doesn't have all day. If you hurry, we can go take a look at The Point."

"Not today, son," Grandpop said. "This thing's coming fast. Gotta get on the road."

Jeanette Gray Finnegan, Captain Charlie's oldest daughter, finished up her work, took one more look around, and then closed the door and locked it. Luke was now waiting in the doorway of the schoolhouse to help his mother with her papers and books. At the steps of the building, he handed off some of the load to his brother and cousin, and they all walked across the sandy yard to the edge of the woods where Grandpop waited. A worried scowl crossed Captain Charlie's face, a look the children did not often see.

"Comin', Grandpop," Luke called out, and all four of them crawled into the old car.

"Okeydokey, men, let's get 'er on the road. Storm's a-comin.'" Captain Charlie tried to make his eager passengers smile, even though he really needed for them to get a move on and hurry to get home safely and beat the impending winds.

"Grandpop," Ellie said, "the swing was goin' by itself. I hardly had to push it. The wind kept taking it higher and higher."

"Mine was, too, Grandpop. If Luke hadn't come, I would have beat Ellie." Blake wanted his grandfather's attention also. Being the smallest one was not the easiest, but it never really held Blake back. He tried everything that the older kids did.

"What do you hear, Pop?" asked Nett. "Do we have much time? Mr. Austin said it might not be as bad as we think."

"Well, it does seem to be slowing a little. I was over to the Coast Guard station this morning, when we got the latest reports. Looks like it might blow out before it gets to us. Then again, it could go inland. Whatever it does, we need to be ready for any direction it decides to take." Villagers all knew the storm was coming, but where was a mystery, so the islanders had to prepare for an approach from the ocean or the sound, just to be safe.

The ride back to the lighthouse complex was full of chatter: school, storm, who could swing higher, and other challenges, including if Ellie had been teased or picked on that day and what Grandmom Odessa might be fixing for a snack.

This lighthouse family lived separately from the rest of the village. They were out on the beach, a couple of miles east of the village. It was not a problem for the youngsters, as they loved the secluded spot. They lived on the beach. Nobody else could claim that. Plus they had each other for built-in friends.

Life was a little more complicated for Ellie than the other two, because the young girls of the village sometimes joined together to pick on her about not having parents, a jab the mean kids liked to use if they found themselves bored and jealous of the beautiful little sandy-haired child. However, they didn't dare to disrespect Luke. He was the coolest boy on the elementary side of the school. He was good-looking, smart, and the best athlete, and he had just been given the lead in the upcoming play, *Tom Sawyer*. Blake made up in attitude what he lacked in age and size, and for some reason he was the favorite of all the girls in his classroom.

Ellie's full name was Eleanor Wilson Gray, and she was her grandmother and Grandpop's charge since birth. Her mother and father were both dead. Her father was swept out to sea about three months before Ellie was born, in just such a storm, while trying to secure a fastening for the Diamond Shoals lightship, which sat anchored on one of the underwater mountains. The lightship was a second beacon, attached to a disabled ship permanently secured to the area just in case bad weather prevented vessels from seeing the light from the lighthouse on shore. These shoals had claimed hundreds of cargo-laden ships before the government stepped in to create a beacon that served to warn them to steer around the area. Trying to maneuver through the three sand mountains as a shortcut was tempting but too dangerous, and mariners were not willing to lose their ship or lives over it.

Ellie's mother, Annie, was Captain Charlie's youngest daughter, and she had been sickly all her life. Even though Annie was pregnant, she never got over the loss of her husband, and in her grief she refused to leave her bed. In this weakened condition she could not manage the strength to survive childbirth. She died while giving birth to her daughter. At Annie's death, it was up to Captain Charlie and his wife to name the fragile newborn, take her home, and raise her as their own. They chose the name, and almost immediately everyone called her "Ellie." Keeping her was the greatest pleasure the old couple had. They lost two and gained one, and the one was very special.

★ 2 ★

You Live Where?

The compound occupied several acres of land on which stood the 208-foot tower known as the Cape Hatteras Lighthouse. Along with the tower, two lodges located near the structure housed the keeper, his assistants, and their families. Captain Charlie lived in the smaller of the two residences. The larger of the two was a duplex with separate entrances, double fireplaces, and room enough to house the two assistants along with their families. Near the two buildings were several outbuildings used to maintain the working structure. One was a barn to shelter the two government horses and the wagon they pulled. Another building was an enclosed garage to give cover to the automobile that the keeper and his assistants used. This building also served as a storage and maintenance area for items used in keeping up the grounds and a work house for the lighthouse crew. Even with an enclosed garage, the salt still crept in to wreak havoc on the metal of the car. Captain Charlie was one of the few on the island with an automobile, and it looked like a piece of junk because of the salt air eating away at the finish. Ellie and Blake loved to sit in the front seat along with Grandpop and stare at the floorboard. They would watch the sandy road speed by through the rusted-out holes in the bottom of the old Ford.

In addition to official outbuildings, located off the back of the main quarters was Grandmom's chicken coop. This structure was also enclosed. On the beach, this close to the ocean, even chickens needed somewhere sturdy to stay.

Here and there around the acreage grew scrub oaks, yaupon, and pine, cedar, juniper, and cypress trees. Also on the property were fig trees, a mulberry tree, blackberry patches, multiple grapevines, and as many flowering bushes as Grandmom could find in the village to transplant on the property. She was constantly trading items to other women in the community for cuttings from rose bushes, hydrangea bushes, and hedge, which now surrounded the porch and walkways. The complex was beautiful, with grass growing around the tower and near the house. Keeping the shifting sand away was hard, but Grandmom gave it her best, and some stretches had spots that looked like a normal yard.

A baseball field, built by the Coast Guard, occupied the place between the lightkeepers and the wooded area that separated the lighthouse compound from the Coast Guard station. The villages came together here to play against each other and the Coast Guard team. Every Sunday in the summer, there was a game. The rivalry between the villages was fierce, spilling over into conversation on Mondays. Those Sundays were the most fun. Everyone in the adjoining localities came to this side of the island for picnics and bragging rights. The dirt roads and clearings around the lighthouse were crowded with old jalopies, cars, slat-railed tall trucks, and horses hitched to trees, loosed from their wagons, or tied to the wagon they pulled. All vehicles arrived loaded with good things to eat. The women planned their menus while at church (hopefully not during the preacher's sermon). Baskets included fried chicken, fried fish, deviled eggs, and breadstuffs. Many women made cakes and casseroles and pots of tea, which filled out the community fare. Luke, Ellie, and

Blake considered these special days as personal delights because people came to their house for games and fun.

Luke and Blake lived in the large lodge that housed the assistant light-keepers. Their father, Bill Finnegan, was married to Captain Charlie's oldest daughter, Jeanette—also known as Nett. Bill was employed by the navy to help maintain the light. This lodge was inland of the main quarters and was twice as large. It was built to accommodate two assistants and their families, but at this time only one family occupied the space—which provided a huge area to play in, and the kids took advantage of it. The proximity of the keepers and the Coast Guardsmen allowed the two agencies to work closely together to keep islanders and ships at sea as safe as they could be.

The three children felt fortunate to live on the government base where the lighthouse stood. They had never lived near the stores or churches or other boys and girls. They lived here—with each other and with the seamen from the Coast Guard station. Every day was exciting.

As they came away from the village, Grandpop turned right. The ocean was visible in front, and the lighthouse stood tall at the end of the long, sandy, two-track road. Everybody loved the sight of the tower rising majestically in the distance, with its perfectly painted white and black spiral stripes. The lighthouse had last been hand painted by Bill and one of Captain Charlie's sons, Wallace. They hung from the top in a wooden staging area with slats enclosing the sides, protecting them from falling off. Ropes on the top railing of the tower were fastened to the box, and others were tied to stakes on the ground. Men from town volunteered to take turns spotting the two, hoping to avoid an accident. The children watched daily from the porch of the assistant keepers' lodge.

As the old jalopy neared home, the two youngest stretched on tiptoes, leaning far out the windows of the backseat, straining to see the sky and hoping they could glimpse the storm. To their disappointment, all looked pretty calm. The gusts of wind were few and weak, and the sky looked like every cloud had been sucked away to join their friends at the top of a very angry storm. It was literally the calm before the storm. Everything was visible and fresh. The wind and clouds had gone to be collected with all the other bad weather but would soon return with a furor to smite them. "Smite" was a word that Grandpop used when he stood in front of the church and talked about the devil. Blake was always saying, "If you don't be careful, something will smite you!" This seemed to be his biggest threat. Now the storm was going to smite them all. *Uh-oh!*

As the car rounded the corner and the pond back of the quarters came into view, they noticed that the turtles, usually there to greet them with their silly necks craning up to say welcome home, were gone.

"Where'd all the turtles go, Grandpop?" asked Blake.

"Oh, they're hiding someplace. You can depend on that, son," said Grandpop. "All the animals are shoring up a hiding place. They are smart when it comes to what nature is doing, and they smell trouble. They've seen it before."

"Even the wolves?" Blake asked again, just to make sure Grandpop meant "all."

"The wolves most of all. They are already in the woods, probably rounding up all the rabbits."

"Why the rabbits?" Blake questioned, beginning to make Grandpop wish he had worded things differently.

Luke jumped in to save Grandpop and shot back, "To eat them!" and he cut his eyes sideways at Blake beside him.

"Noooo!" said Blake and Ellie in chorus. "Is that true, Grandpop?"

"No. Now leave your grandpop alone!" Nett snapped. "He has enough on his mind without you three hounding him. Anyway, I'll bet Grandmom has some treats for this afternoon. Those Coast Guard boys will be working up an appetite."

"Me, too," said Blake.

It seemed at times that they all lived in the keeper's quarters, because there was so much going on, and Grandmom was in charge of the whole lot of them. Along with Ellie, Jack, the youngest of the keeper's sons, was in and out as he went to and from college. All of the other Gray siblings lived in the village—married, with jobs and their own houses.

Captain Charlie had eight children. Jeanette, the oldest, lived next door with her husband, Bill, and their two sons: Luke, twelve, and Blake, seven. Fatio, known as Fay, the oldest boy, was away most of the time serving in the Merchant Marines. Wallace was in the Coast Guard, learning Morse code and radar technology in Norfolk, Virginia. When he was on the island he was at the Loran Station working the wireless at a lonely outpost near the beach. Tommy ran the grocery store, which had been in the family for years. He was married to Winnie, who was also a schoolteacher. Iva, the second daughter, lived in Winston-Salem with her husband and children. The next-to-youngest son was Curtis. He was also in the Coast Guard but stationed in New York, where he met and married a beautiful Cuban girl whom he named "Pete," because he didn't like her name, Carmelito. Curtis, a small-town boy, was hesitant about explaining that name to other islanders, so he called her something else. The entire family also fell in love with the charming, Spanish-speaking, dark-haired lovely. When Pete was on the island, Grandpop finally had a translator for what the radio was indicating, as most of the reception was from Cuba and in Spanish. The island picked up a majority of the radio airwaves from the Caribbean island, and it was sometimes necessary to pay attention to the anxiety in the announcer's voice rather than what he said.

Of course, included in the eight had been the youngest daughter, Annie—Ellie's mother, who had died giving birth to Ellie.

Pete walked into the keeper's quarters one Christmas wearing a beautiful red tam. Fatio grabbed the small woolen hat, blew his nose in the middle of it, handed it back, and said, "Don't ever wear that silly hat again!" and they both laughed so hard, she forgot why she was there.

Pete was learning the island, and having brothers of her own she was comfortable with the pranks they pulled on their new sister-in-law. It actually made her feel like a true member of the family. Of course, if Curtis had been there, it would have been an invitation to a tussle. With that many brothers, trouble was always in the making. It was either a scuffle or a contest to see who could walk on their hands the longest. Fay won every time, as he could walk down the stairs. Game over!

The clan was large, but so were most island families: the Millers, Jennettes, Barnettes, Midgetts, Farrows, Scarboroughs, and others. Large families made it fun when they all got together, and there were a lot of opportunities for gatherings. Island people worked hard and tried to play harder. The inhabitants lived a solitary existence, away from the mainland and deprived of many conveniences afforded to those living off island, but they would not have it any other way. They were also a very relaxed people. Everybody knew everybody else. The drawbacks to island life were not noticeable to the locals but very unusual to persons off island.

As the jalopy slowed to a stop near the house, all three children rushed to the porch, which spread across the front of the house. Blake jumped into the long three-seater swing hanging from the heavy beams and pushed off, not waiting for Ellie, who was headed in that direction. Luke hit the ground running, threw his books down on the church bench on the porch, and took off after Grandpop, not to miss one moment of these exciting days. He also knew his dad would be waiting for Pop to come home, and that is where Luke wanted to be—in on the action, near his dad, and trying to stay quiet so that they would not send him home. Ellie crawled onto the swing beside Blake, and both were like jumping beans, their feet kicking and the tickle-punching filling the air with giggles, snorts, and squealing.

At ten years old Ellie was between Luke and Blake in age. Being the middle child she was grown up enough to talk to Luke and silly enough to hang with Blake.

Grandmom came to the porch with a towel covering a plate. "Cookies!" squealed Blake, and once more the race was on.

⋆ 3 ★

A Hurricane Story

Preparing for a hurricane was second nature to Luke and Ellie. They had experienced a strong one of exciting consequences when Luke was seven and Ellie was almost five. Back then, the anticipated storm was supposed to be one of the worst. The local men began talking about it while sitting around Mr. Ephram's store listening to the radio. Bill had brought back to the island a special radio he had purchased overseas while on active duty in the navy. It had a shortwave component that allowed reception from several foreign countries. The storm was moving up the coast slowly and picking up wind speed over the warm waters of the Gulf Stream. Captain Charlie, son Tommy, son-in-law Bill, and brother-in-law Baxter were among the men in the store. Baxter was married to Josephine Gray, Charlie's sister, and there was a strong bond between the two men. They were as close as if they were real brothers, not brothers by marriage. Charlie had one brother, Cyrus, and two sisters, and they married men that he quite approved of. For instance, Baxter was one of the few surfmen who was issued the Congressional Medal of Honor for Lifesaving—for the many times he risked his own life to save others.

Charlie, Baxter, and Tommy had built a shrimp boat in Baxter's backyard, located on the hill leading down to the sound. The ridge dropped down in the back to the waters of the sound, and the plan was to roll the finished vessel down the hill on the logs of trees that were cut down to clear a path for the boat to be moved to the water. A channel was dredged out to get the craft to the nearest cove. The boat was now within sight of Baxter's house, resting in a deepwater canal that Captain Bernice owned. The Landing, as Bernice's creek was called, was also where the mail boat came in, loaded with all sorts of supplies and necessary provisions for the natives. The depth was dredged out pretty deep, as that boat drew a heavy draft.

All of the men in the store were friends, most having served at one time or another in the Coast Guard, thus giving them the title of the rank they earned while in service. Captain Bernice was an avid fisherman and a hauler of freight. He had dredged out the huge canal leading up to his property for both his boat and the mail boat. The inlet was large enough for other local men to also moor their boats. Boats were tied to both sides of the channel. Some were small personal skiffs for pound netting, while others were larger fishing vessels that traveled down the sound to the large inlet between Hatteras and Ocracoke that provided access to the ocean. It was fun to go down to the docks in the evening to see what catch the local fishermen brought in each day. Families waited there to buy the fresh fish, oysters, and clams that filled the small boats. The larger boats deposited their haul at the commercial docks in Hatteras.

Most familiar to every kid in Buxton was the wide dock at the mouth of the landing built to accommodate the government mail boat. Most of them had learned to swim there. No one came into that area who did not anticipate jumping off that dock into the warm waters of the canal to enjoy a day of swimming. When kids came to the dock and did not jump, then somebody threw them over, and it was sink or swim. The fact that nobody drowned during this ritual was a miracle, but strangely, the dog paddle must have been natural to humans and dogs, because it saved many a soul. Since all of this was widespread knowledge, parents made sure they were the ones who introduced their children to the Landing dock and taught them to swim on their own. Uncle Jack and his cousin Lindy, Baxter's son, taught Luke and Ellie.

Because of the depth, smaller kids did not swim to the middle of the canal. They mostly played around the sandy shoreline that the dredged-up bottom had created. There was so much sand, bleached white by the sun, that it created a rather large beach. It was one of the areas, like the lighthouse, where residents of Buxton came to enjoy a day of picnics and water activities.

Out in the sound, not very far from the mouth of the canal, was another huge mountain of sand, deposits from the deep trenched inlet that had been carved out. Locals called this small sandy island Gull Island, as it was occupied by hundreds of screeching seagulls and their nests. This raised knoll was a favorite place for picnics. Most would use one of the small craft tied to the docks at Bernice's landing and either row or pole out to the area for a day of fishing, catching minnows, using a dip net for crabs in the shallow waters, or just wading. Going out to Gull Island meant a special day.

This day, Captain Charlie, Tommy, and Baxter's sons Lindy and Cantwell went to work securing the boat, named the *Odessa W*, after the wives. Naming a boat after one's wife meant good luck and return to the island's fishermen. Josephine refused to have her name on the vessel. She was still smarting from almost losing her husband to the waters of the Atlantic, and she hated the thought of Baxter going out to sea, even for fun.

In anticipation of the storm, Charlie moved his family to Baxter's house for safe keeping. At that time, the men were not sure if the hurricane would approach the area from the sound or the sea. They only knew the storm was coming, and it was headed straight toward Cape Hatteras Island. Charlie was not willing to take the chance that it would come from the sea, where the huge waves from the storm surge would breach the dunes and strand them on the beach at the lighthouse. Captain Charlie and Bill stayed at the keeper's quarters to protect and do damage control to the lighthouse and surrounding properties, feeling comfortable that their families were out of harm's way.

All of the excitement of the coming storm was not lost on Luke and Ellie. They were not afraid, though. They had been through storms before, but they were young enough to be unaware of the true dangers of such a feat of nature. As children they just got into the spirit of the quick movements of the adults as all went about their duties preparing for the nasty weather.

The storm gradually crept in—strong winds and rain, giving way to stronger winds and more rain—and the house shook with the gusts. Everyone tried to keep a cheery mood by singing and telling stories. But even as Nett played familiar songs on the piano, she kept being interrupted by people rushing around for pans to catch the water coming down through the roof, as shingles popped off almost with the rhythm of the piano. The storm lasted a day and a half. At one point, Ellie and Luke went out on Uncle Baxter's huge porch, sat in rocking chairs, put their feet up, and let the moving house rock the chairs. Uncle Baxter's house was well sheltered, located on a hill and surrounded by huge live oak and poplar trees. The porch wrapped around the entire house, a style common among houses in the village, and the front portion was screened in as a guard against the summertime mosquitoes. The screens began to split and flap around in the wind. Still, it was fun to hold on to the sides of the large rockers and steel themselves against the gusts of wind that regularly swayed the house.

At one point, Luke said, "Ellie, listen!"

They both held their breaths and listened, only to hear a loud cracking noise, and then another, even louder than the first. Almost together, they jumped out of the rocking chairs and rushed back into the house to warn the grown-ups

"The house is giving way!" shouted Luke.

"It is! Uncle Baxter . . . It is!" cried Ellie. "We heard it!" she wailed as she pulled on the old man's sleeve. Baxter's sons jumped up to see what the children were so excited about, followed closely by Jack, who had also moved to the house to be closer to the sound in case he was needed to help keep the boat tied. The women in the room were in obvious shock at the news and moved with the others toward the porch door.

This house was one of the sturdiest on the island. Its foundations and most of the pilings were of strong ships' timber, salvaged from the wrecks that frequently washed up on the beach, either from being stranded on Diamond Shoals or having lost their way during storms. For this house to break apart in even the strongest of storms would mean all houses on the island were in jeopardy. What they saw when they got to the porch was the huge live oak tree, there since any of them could remember, leaning to the left, with a portion of its mighty roots showing. They all stood there and watched in wonder as each heavy gust of wind coming from the southwest showed more and more of the gigantic root system coming out of the earth, until the massive tree finally crashed solidly to the ground.

Nett, holding little Blake, teared up as did Baxter's wife, Josephine, and Odessa. It was heartbreaking to see that old tree go. They remembered all the birds that had built their nests over the years, the squirrels, and the brothers, cousins, and their friends practicing with their air rifles, shooting at the crows that kept a steady chatter during the day. All of this would be missed. The wind and rain seemed to get stronger. Huge gusts were rocking the house, and the solid downpour of rain was now slashing sideways.

"You children get inside. I must have been crazy to let you come out here. What if that tree had fallen this way, on the house, or even just the porch? You would be dead! Now don't ask to come out here again! This is not a game. This is one of nature's angriest ways of expressing herself, and you had better respect that!" Nett was trying to control her own fear while instilling a little in the children. This was a dangerous time, and they needed to acknowledge the peril surrounding them.

Quietly the children and adults moved back to the living room and their quest of keeping out the rain, which had picked up and was now pounding the sides of the house.

Luke and Ellie decided to go upstairs, away from the adults, and watch the storm from the front bedroom window. When they were stretched on their bellies across the bed looking at the storm's fury, they looked at each other and giggled. They had seen something spectacular and had gotten away with only a scolding. They talked and snickered about things for a while longer, and then realized the wind had begun to die down. They stared at the fallen oak and watched the spindly poplar trees bending almost to the ground, only to bounce back when the gust passed. Every tree struggled, and the bushes lost their leaves with each strong blast.

Then they saw a figure making his way to the house. The man was staggering back and forth against the wind blasts, holding on to a fence or a tree limb, trying to keep his feet under him. He had on a khaki baseball cap with side flaps pulled way down. The insignia on his hat was a heavily braided Coast Guard disk. He had on a thick yellow surf slicker and heavy black boots. The wind gusts began to get further and further apart, as the blowing became less steady. As the rain slowed a bit, it turned into a steady pour. The storm was winding down, and somebody was coming. Luke and Ellie slid off the bed, hit the floor, and took off, racing downstairs to announce that the storm was over and company was arriving. The front door flew open, and a massive, drenched old man stood in the doorway.

"Alright, boys!" announced Captain Bernice in a booming voice. "Baxter, round 'em up. The eye is a-gettin' ready to pass over, and we need to get to the creek and check them boats! Hurry, we only have about thirty to forty-five minutes before the back side of this monster comes at us again." Captain Bernice was concerned about the *Odessa W*, but he also needed help shoring up his huge freight hauler, which was large enough to carry a car—if you could figure out how to get it on the deck. The captain needed more than one strong hand, and it would have to be a massive, calloused one to match his two. He was a tall, burly man. He knew he could get help from the crew of rangy guys at the Miller household.

Baxter and the boys began to pull on their boots and heaviest foul-weather gear, and head toward the door,

"Mommy!?"

"Aunt Nett!" followed in echo. Ellie snapped her head around at Luke and mimicked what he said. She wanted to do what he said, whatever that was going to be, giving strength to the argument Luke was about to put up.

"Can't we go? There isn't any wind, and the rain has stopped. We just want to watch," said Luke. He had automatically included Ellie, as they were sidekicks. Luke could smell an adventure. Something was in the air.

"Heavens, no!" said Nett, but Jack and Lindy stopped her. The two young men were used to being stuck with these children. They actually enjoyed it, teasing them, playing one off the other, and seeing things through their eyes and setting them laughing all the time. Also, they were good gofers who would fetch anything, like well-trained dogs, and the boys loved them.

"It's okay, Miss Nett," said Lindy. "We'll take care of them. It doesn't take all of us to tie up the boats, and most of the men are already down there."

"It's fine, Sis. Lindy and I will hold on to them. This is something they should see," said Jack, catching hold of Nett's arm. "We'll be careful and come back as soon as we've had a look."

Uncle Jack was their favorite uncle before, but now he had risen to the status of a Greek god. *Oooooooh, this is gonna be fun,* they both thought.

Ellie raced to put on her new white rubber "majorette boots," as she called them—the ones Uncle Bill had bought her when he was on the mainland. The children got dressed the fastest ever, in fear they would miss the adventure.

Luke squeezed Ellie's hand tightly and said, "Don't let go of me, Ellie. We need to keep up. I bet nobody gets to do this," Lindy grabbed one kid, Jack the other, and out the door they all went.

Lindy and Jack ran so fast to catch the men that the two smaller ones couldn't keep their feet on the ground. They felt like they were flying. Everybody was out of breath as they breached the top of the hill that hid the sound from the road. At the top they stared down at the docks at the most amazing sight any of them had ever witnessed. There was a huge gully where the water used to be. The eye of the hurricane had swirled around so tightly that all the water had been sucked out of the sound and into the ocean. Ellie thought it looked like a picture in Grandpop's Bible of the parting of the Red Sea, when Moses crossed over with the Israelites. She put her hand over her open mouth, and when she finally tore her eyes away she looked up at Luke. His face was drained of color, his mouth was dropped open, and he was speechless. They ran down the road that led to the dock and stood beside the men. They had also taken a shocked step back but quickly gained their composure. Not only was the water gone, but all the boats, tied so tightly, were hanging from the moorings—stuck to the middle of the pole and just dangling there. The water was gone. The only thing holding them up were the ropes tied firmly to the stakes.

Out in the distance, Gull Island looked like a mountain in the middle of a green desert. Without the water around it, it looked huge. Everything was dead calm—no gulls screaming, no water lapping, all the sound grass that usually stood tall under the water was lying flat on the waterless ground, sort of bubbling. This was a sight!

Finally Captain Bernice spoke. "Well, boys, nothing to do here. Boats are tight, don't seem to be harmed. We got about thirty or so minutes 'til the water comes back. When that eye swings back around, we better be sheltered. What say we walk out to Gull Island?"

Luke's heart skipped a beat, and Ellie's picked up. She turned flush as she once again clapped her hand over her gaping mouth and rolled her eyes at Luke as if to say, "Uh-oh," followed by a musical "OooooooOoooh."

All the men looked at each other and began to walk toward the huge valley left by the water being sucked out to sea.

Lindy said, "Pop, can we take the kids? Jack and I will hold on to them. We want to go, too."

"Guess we have to take them," Baxter said. "Not much danger 'til the storm comes back, and we'll know that when the water starts creeping up around our feet. We'll feel the wind when it starts to blow again, then we'll head for home. But I ain't never seen nothing like this, and I don't intend to miss it. You boys wanted to bring them kids, so keep a hand onto them, and let's get goin.'"

Everybody had on boots, and they slowly started feeling their way down the embankment into the flat grass, on their way to the huge mountain in front of them. Ellie could hear the bubbles burst under the grass, sounding like crabs in a bushel basket talking about crawling all over each other to get out. The men were laughing and starting to tell the tales they would embellish in the future as everybody picked their way forward.

Ellie and Luke were closest to the ground, both staring at what they saw trapped in the grass at their feet.

"Look, Luke," said Ellie. "A little shrimp, and look! What's that?"

Jack looked down and said, "Lindy, look-a-here. Ain't never seen one that small!"

Lindy said, "I'll be dang. It's an octopus, but it ain't bigger than an inch. Lookee here, Pop. Ever seen one this small?"

Baxter took the small creature in his hand. "I'll be! Looks like everything lives in these waters. Don't have much to eat so they don't get big 'til they get to the ocean. Unless something bigger eats them before they get there."

Caught in the grass were hundreds of small creatures. Shrimp, octopi, clams, families of tiny minnows, oysters, very small crabs, and larger ones not able to untangle themselves from the weeds—all squirming and wiggling to make their way through the flattened undergrowth without benefit of water. The children and adults were fascinated. About halfway to the new mountain, the water began to seep back in.

"Better turn 'round, boys!" said Captain Bernice. "Looks like she's a-comin' back! Wind's picking up a little. Let's get a move on!"

The party of men and two young-uns started back to the shore. Lindy and Jack grabbed the two wide-eyed children and picked up the pace. Younger and faster, they knew they were responsible for the safety of these munchkins, and it had already been an exciting day. When they got to shore, the boys started to trot toward the woods behind Lindy's house, taking the shortcut home.

Just as everybody got back, the wind began to gust again. This time, they saw Captain Bernice grab on to a tree branch to keep from getting blown over as he made his way down the road to his house. The storm was mad, and it was going to get madder. The back side of the storm was always worse than the front. But everybody was safe, and there were puddles to clean up in the house as the shingles began popping again from the furious gusts that blew on the back side of the store.

If they made it past the strongest part of this storm, they would be all right. But what a tale they would all tell—about "the parting of the Pamlico Sound"—and everyone had already started, relating their versions all at once. The two little ones went back upstairs.

★ 4 ★

We Need Water!

The next day, back at the keeper's quarters, the children checked out the damage done to their house. Luke and his mother helped his father, Bill, next door in the long lodge beside the captain's quarters. There had not been much concern for this house, as Bill spent all of his time trying to secure first one thing then another with the lighthouse. He and Captain Charlie had paid little attention to what was happening at home. Their job was the Cape Hatteras Light. They had seen only one ship struggling to fight the storm, and that ship was dangerously close to land—close enough that it could be seen. The ship did not send a distress signal, so nobody launched a surfboat after it. The vessel kept bobbing around until the wind blew it in the right direction.

Captain Charlie had called the Coast Guard, and the seamen arrived with two of the big government horses pulling a dory. They were ready to launch if need be. All stood on the dunes soaking wet. No matter the yellow slickers of the Coast Guard, the sand blasting from a full-on hurricane made a man feel naked against the fury of the blow. They tried to hold on to the horses in order to stand erect, and they watched the floundering ship. With each gust the boys were blown sideways, jerking them away from the horses shielding them from the most severe blasts. The horses had on heavy blinders, protection against both biting sand spray and the foamy wet onslaught of the breakers, should they have to breach them in order to launch. They stood solid against the bombardment, ready if needed.

At the same time, it became more necessary to keep checking the light. Captain Charlie and Bill were inside the beacon, protecting the lenses, which were delicate. The wind was fierce. Keeping the light in good repair was essential as this weather continued into the night.

Ships could navigate by sight, but the light was needed should a ship venture to come through when it was too dark to see the shore. Being blown into the shoals in this weather was certain disaster. Everybody was on alert. Captain Charlie watched from his lookout post.

When it appeared the ship would navigate safely past the shoals, the men left the surfboat near the dune until the weather broke, took the horses to the keeper's barn, and temporarily secured them. They then put their heads down against the weather and, leaning forward against the wind and driving rain, struggled to make it inside the lighthouse in order to study the storm from there. The structure did not even creak. The blasts of wind and the sheets of water only made a sound against the windows scattered up the spiral staircase, and at the top, the swirling hurricane was something to watch. The seamen were not regretting how wet they had gotten while dragging those horses around, because to be at the top of the Cape Hatteras Light in the middle of one of the strongest storms to hit the capes in years was something they could tell their families about when they got back home.

The houses were a mess. The window facing off the back of Luke's room had been blown out, and there was glass to be cleaned up. There was no water. The cisterns had stopped pumping, and even the underground pressure was affected. Nett made Bill take Luke's mattress out on the porch to air out. Luke was assigned to watch Blake and was also trying to bring water to his mom from the rain barrel at the side of the house. They had thrown open all the windows to get out the musty smell of what could be mildew if it wasn't mopped up in a hurry, and Blake was getting into everything.

Hurricanes sometimes required more clean-up after the wind and water damage subsided. This family had their hands full, and with the failing cisterns not having the pressure to pump water to the surface, the rain barrels were getting low.

The cistern at the keeper's quarters was also in disrepair, not pumping from the old iron-handled pumps that were located in the house, kitchen, back porch, and various places across the yard, especially the barn. The cistern, a waterproof receptacle, was usually a huge box, big like a closet turned on its side and buried half underground, with a couple of feet of the cement structure showing above ground. It was lined with something waterproof—could even be heavy paint or plastic lining—to keep the water clean. It was supplied with water either by rain running down a pipe from the ceiling and roof edges of the house, or by a pump in the ground that allowed occupants to fill the cistern from groundwater. There was no such thing as public water south of the mainland.

All cisterns used on the island had elaborate filters at the top of the opening to keep out debris, insects, and animals. The filters were cleaned regularly if the water was to be used for cooking or drinking. The long-handled pumps that sucked the water out of the cistern were attached to filters also. Water pressure was the key to getting water from the container to the pump next to a sink or barrel. The cisterns near the house were filled mostly by rainwater. Drinking water was the best if it came from the rain.

After the storm, the atmospheric pressure from the winds and the severe sucking out of the water that a hurricane used to fuel its fury had overridden the ground pressure, and the hand pumps just pumped air.

Most island families also kept rain barrels at the corners of the house, with gutters running along the roof to catch the rain and direct it down to the barrel below. These also had screens over them to keep out dirt and insects. Grandmom and Jeanette used their rain barrels for watering plants and filling the troughs for the pigs, chickens, cow, and horses.

After a storm, both Grandmom Odessa and Nett would dip water from the rain barrels and bring the water into the house to boil, for use in cooking and washing until the pumps could be primed to bring up water from the cisterns. The water was heavy, and they needed so much of it. Dealing with the apparently dry cisterns was becoming quite a chore. This scene was probably played out all over the island. But the only alternative was living on the mainland, where city water was supplied, and who wanted to do that? Everyone agreed that living on the island was different, but it was worth the trouble. They were quite satisfied to deal with their problems in exchange for the sand, sea, clean air, beautiful cloud-filled sky, fishing, and island life they all experienced.

After a long day of hauling water, cleaning, repairing, and getting their lives back in working order, everyone was tired. Grandmom insisted that Ellie have a bath. Here was another problem. Ellie usually took a bath in a huge tub on the back porch when weather permitted. When it did not, she climbed into an old wooden tub carried into the warm kitchen, which was filled with water from the pump at the edge of the sink and heated for comfort. Neither was available on this night. So Grandmom hoisted little Ellie to the edge of the sink, with her feet dangling over the side, and began to give her a sponge bath with water Grandpop had carried in from the rain barrel. Ellie put her feet into the sink and began playing with the handle of the useless pump beside her. Up and down, up and down went the handle of the pump, making the most irritating clanging noise. She just worked that pump and Grandmom's nerves 'til Miss Odessa just couldn't take it anymore. This had been a long day, and Grandmom was getting a headache.

Grandpop yelled from the other room, "Odessa, get that young-un off that pump. I can't even hear myself think!"

"Child, let go of that handle," said Grandmom. "You are driving me crazy! It doesn't work, and you are going to break it if you don't quit yanking at it."

Ellie gave the pump handle one more push, and this time some water dribbled out. Grandmom's eyes got so big that she turned to Ellie and, in a little voice—almost a whisper, so as not to let Grandpop hear her—said, "Honey, do it again. This time harder." Ellie gave the handle all the strength she had, and out gushed the water.

"Charlie Gray, get in here!" Grandmom demanded. "I think this child has fixed the pump!"

Ellie was then pumping and pumping as hard as she could, and the water was just pouring out. She and Grandmom were laughing up a storm when Grandpop came in.

"My lord, young-un, you've done it! Yippee!" he hollered, and he started dancing a jig right there in the kitchen. "Lordy, Lordy, Lordy!" he praised. "We got water, you've done pumped up the pressure!"

All the next day, Ellie and Luke went from pump to pump until their little arms were so sore they could hardly move, getting water out of the ground. Uncle Jack had a go at it, and Bill was relentless. Even Jeanette gave it a try. Water! How truly wonderful!

When they were too tired to pump anymore, the kids turned their attention to the best game of all: Jump the cistern. The cement cistern was about two feet from the edge of the back porch, and as a little one, two feet looked like ten feet, so the game was to see who had the nerve to jump from the porch to the cistern. Ellie had watched Luke do it for years, but she was afraid to try it. She was not supposed to be bruised, and if she missed, not only would she have marks from hitting the cement box, she would probably knock out her teeth. But she was finally not afraid of the box. She had conquered the inside of the house, and now it was time to see how she did outside the house. Luke was daring her, and nobody was around, or this little scene would not be playing out.

Ellie started and balked. She started again and came up just short of the edge, stretching out her arms, making little circles to keep from falling. Once more, this time she landed on her feet, not her teeth, and the game was on. They jumped until it was no longer a challenge. Then they spied Grandpop heading toward the lighthouse steps. They both saw him at the same time and raced to just short of his knees, and just short of bumping into him. They followed like tin soldiers in line behind him, marching with their knees high, tailing him up the steps and into the foyer of the tower. They spent the next hour seeing who could run up the lighthouse steps the most times. They would sleep well tonight.

★ 5 ★

Mr. O'Neal's Couch

This new storm headed their way was highly anticipated for Ellie and Luke, as they wondered what unusual problem this one would present. They hurried along, helping to prepare for the coming wind and rain. Everybody worked quickly to shore things up. Blake knew that he was now old enough to be included in any adventure that might decide to show its face. He was the same age as Luke was when he walked with the grown-ups down to Bernice's landing to tie up the boats. Blake, as usual, got most animated when he talked about "What if?" Since this was not anybody's first hurricane, as they came every year, they all knew the dangers of wind and tide.

Everybody quickly removed anything from the yard that could fly away, storing some things under the house, putting other things in the barn, and feeling sorry for the chickens. Jack was responsible for making the coop safe against the wind. Then they could only hope the chickens, who had names, survived. Even the fowl sensed the weather change. They were all hiding up in the rafters of the roof. The birds were gone. There was no sign of animals, not even the long-eared rabbit who made his home on the grounds of the compound. Everybody had taken cover.

The two huge government horses were of great concern. They were plow horses, with beautiful long manes and tails, and lots of hair down the shanks of their legs. Their hoofs were wide and made huge divots in the ground when they walked. Running, they almost left holes, their legs were so powerful. One was mostly dusty black, and the other was brown. They were bigger than other horses, but they were the only horses the children knew and they were all friends. Grandpop decided to move them to a bigger barn, the one on the Coast Guard property. There they would have a sturdier stable, more people to take care of them, and most important, the other horses would keep his two calm. The sounds of powerful wind gusts pounding the sides of the barn would likely spook the horses if they were left alone, so Grandpop set about preparing the horses for the move.

Being different from most, these unusual steeds needed special attention. Lots of people had wild ponies that they trained, or riding horses to pull their wagons and heavy loads, or just for traveling around the island. The animals ran free on the land at that point in time, with only a mark behind their ear for identification. Usually a person showed up at the back door and gave a whistle, and the horse trotted over. Horses and cows rambled around the island eating grass or straw, keeping near their own house. This brand of horse, provided by the government, was kept enclosed, as when they were needed, they had to be in a given place, not roaming around.

Grandpop and the Coast Guard both had barns for the surf horses. Their mission was to haul boats. They were used when ships were in trouble on the shoals or stranded in the surf. They could be hooked up to the vessel struggling in the wash and bring it in. They had been responsible for saving many a craft from breaking up in the pounding surf, just shy of the shore, as their wide hoofs gave a better grip on the sinking sand and provided them strong pulling power. Most of the time they were harnessed to the dories that men needed to haul down to the beach for rowing out to the stricken ship. Horses were the only transport the rescue team could use to tow a heavy surfboat to the water and not get stuck in the sand or surf. Sometimes the weather was so fierce that the Coast Guard needed their four horses plus Captain Charlie's two to pull a loaded rescue vessel down to the beach. So, Old Tony and Big Roy were friends with the horses they would be bedded down with, and the men who handled them. If needed during a storm, they would already be in place to help.

Grandpop and Bill began to get the horses ready for the move. Whenever anyone went near the horses, the children were not far behind. They looked at the big animals as friends and were sometimes allowed to ride them around the keeper's grounds.

"Grandpop," Luke said, "let us take one. We are used to it, and we can all of us ride Ol' Tony. Please, Daddy. You will be with us. You can ride Big Roy."

"And how are we all going to get back, or have you figured that out, too?" Bill smiled at the look of anticipation on the faces of all three.

"Grandpop can follow us in the car," said Luke with a sense of satisfaction at his grand plan.

Captain Charlie shook his head knowingly, a big smile spread across his face. He closed his eyes, clicked the air with his cheek, and waited for Bill's answer.

Actually, they both had already discussed this very same plan and were pretty impressed that Luke was crafty enough to come up with it. Maybe the kids had discussed it also. Who knows? Whatever happened, it needed to happen now. As Captain Charlie would say, "Time's a-wastin.'"

"Get your harness ready and all of you climb up on that fence. Let's get goin,'" said Bill.

Without any questions or extra talking, Ellie and Blake got on the fence, and Luke got the harness, gave it to his father, and took his place on the fence ready to mount the back of the horse. This was exactly what Blake had been waiting for: some action, and him in the middle of it.

"Grandpop! I gotta pee," said Blake.

"Hit the bushes, boy!" said his grandfather. "Guess Ol' Tony isn't gonna want some wet, smelly kid on his back all the way to the station."

Blake hopped down and disappeared in back of the barn while everybody doubled over with laughter. It was funny to see how excited this little boy was. What a pleasure to have him around. Never a dull moment with him. By the time he got back, Luke and Ellie were already on Ol' Tony's back, and he was patiently waiting for the last load to hop on. He was familiar with the weight of the three children and knew that somebody was missing. Bill hoisted Blake behind Ellie, and Blake wrapped his arms around her waist and laid his head on her back. There was lots of love in this little group. What a foursome: Luke the leader, Ellie and Blake waiting for instructions, and Ol' Tony chewing on some imaginary piece of something, bored with all the delay.

Luke grabbed the reins and moved his heels into Ol' Tony's ribs, nudging him forward. Bill was careful not to go too fast on Big Roy. He didn't want to get Ol' Tony in the mood to run, because this was no time to lose those three little goobers. They all meandered down the path to the Coast Guard station, talking and laughing the whole way. A little teasing for Blake—no matter, he loved the attention. Ol' Tony's back was so wide, Blake was having a difficult time concentrating on not slipping off. Ellie had her arms around Luke but had caught up Blake's jacket in her hand at the same time. If he did fall off, he wouldn't hit the ground because of the jacket. She had a good grip on that. Blake was not going to fall off. If nothing else, he would grab the blanket and pull the rest of them off with him. Now there was a plan.

They all arrived safely at the station, and the children got to play around with some of the boys and hang with the other horses in the barn. Everything was so big: the horses, the wooden dory they would pull, the rack with wheels the craft was sitting on. It really did look like it could conquer the breakers hitting the shore about now. Hopefully this rig would survive the heavy surge that would come.

By the time they all got back, the rain was beginning, and there was a slight pickup of wind. They had delivered Grandmom's goodies to the boys at the station. Nett and Jack had stowed away most of what was not tied down, and now it was time to get inside. It was very important that nothing in the yard nor on the porch could be turned into a flying missile when lifted skyward by the strong wind about to hit land. Things could rocket around, breaking windows and damaging anything they hit. Even small items had disappeared from the yard.

Grandmom "Dessa" was worried about her flowers and garden, but there was nothing she could do to protect them. They would just have to fare for themselves. She usually lost some plants to tide and salt water, but she never gave up the fight. She had the advice of all the other ladies in the church circle on how to handle precious roses and hydrangeas, as all the island women had the same things to worry about. The yards of most on the island bloomed with as many beautiful flowers and bushes as the women could plant, and everyone took a great amount of pride in their roses. There was even a concentrated effort to grow an orange tree that would produce fruit. The day that tree lost a blossom and grew a little knot of an orange, it was the end of all bragging rights. Miss Elsie had accomplished the impossible, and as time went on everyone had to try it. She even named her home the Orange Blossom.

Odessa had more work to do than most, however, because circling all of her flower bushes—as well as the walkways leading this way and that—were beautiful conchs and other equally large shells: huge quahog, coral, and giant scallop shells that had washed up, and those had to be taken in for protection. Shells were most important to Odessa Jennette Gray, a part of her history. Captain Charlie had watched many a time as she held a conch to her ear and listened to the sounds from the ocean. On other occasions, it seemed like things out there were talking to her—maybe, maybe not—but Grandpop wondered. Indulging her with beautiful shells was something he liked to do.

This time, they knew from their friends south of Hatteras Island and the Coast Guard that the storm was coming from the sound, so it was just going to be an inconvenience to the beaches. Rough surf was anticipated along with loud noise, but the water was not expected to breach the dunes. They felt certain of that. It would play havoc with the village, and most families moved their belongings to the second story, getting ready for water in their yard or house. Whatever they had that excessive water could damage was moved to higher ground, either in the hilly areas of the village or the yard of someone who lived on a hill. Baxter's yard was most likely already full of cars and wagons, as was the schoolyard. Buxton's back road was higher than the front road and nearer the woods, so their problems took the form of trees falling on houses or blocking the paths and lanes that permitted travel around the village. Hurricanes on Hatteras Island were dangerous, no matter from which direction they blew.

Buxton had the highest elevation above sea level of any of the seven villages. It was the peak and center of the island. People living in Buxton likely had friends from either Hatteras Village or Kinnakeet Village staying with them. Both those villages were in harm's way when a storm came through the sound. They were safe from the ocean but not the sound because they were the lowest parts of the island. One year, Mr. Hooper's store in Kinnakeet washed all the way from its place near the sound clear across the village to the ocean, and after the storm everybody went down to help Mr. Hooper salvage his wares before the waves washed the old store all the way out to sea.

North at Rodanthe, the direction of the wind and water was also important. There was always the possibility of sound tide washing through the villages and the ocean covering the road. The three villages that made up Chicamacomico were Rodanthe, Waves, and Salvo, and they were inhabited by rugged people, mostly fishermen—strong and accustomed to struggle, more so than people in the other villages. This was the home of the real lifesavers. These men had medals to prove their bravery. They were well respected by the others, and they could handle themselves.

Collectively, everybody was ready. Life meant more than property. Families huddled together with their friends—so let the wind blow, let the rain pour. This island was ready for a storm. It was a pattern repeated several times during the season from August through October. Most of the time, the plan worked.

The Gray clan gathered in the main keeper's quarters. Even though the assistant's quarters were larger, Grandpop wanted Grandmom in her own element, around the kitchen and rooms familiar to her. Everybody liked to be together during times like this. This way, Grandmom knew where everyone was, and she didn't have to worry about this one or that one, only about the storm.

All the oil lamps were ready—overhead lamps pulled down from their chains, filled and lit—and they would swing with the sway of the house. Buckets in place for drips, towels for the ones too strange to catch . . . each had a job. The piano was tuned and ready. Grandpop, Bill, and Uncle Jack had updated their deer stories. The crooked foot deer, the deer with only one antler, the littlest deer, the slew foot deer—the deer stories never seemed to end. Nett had her music books at the piano, and Ellie had her recitation of "The Raggedy Man" practiced to perfection. Blake would be doing a dance. He was good at it, and when it was his turn, every single person, including Grandpop, got up to do the jig that Blake taught them. It was really quite a sight, and also a way to move around, work out some energy to relieve the pressures of all that worry. Blake's energy and natural dance ability made Captain Charlie and Odessa glance at each other in the *knowing* that this child carried some Indian blood. Nobody noticed the inner smiles they displayed.

Luke finished the show with his magic tricks. He had a book of tricks Uncle Fay brought back for him from one of his trips, and Luke had worked tirelessly to master the pages in case someone called upon him to perform. Ellie and Blake were glad when it was Luke's turn. They were his victims, and happy to oblige. Grandmom had baked everything she could think of that the children and Grandpop liked, so, "Come on storm, do your worst!" The islanders were ready.

The wind came, at first like the wail of a sorrowful person—low and whiny—or a not-so-sure ghost practicing his *whooooooo*. Ellie sat quietly in her room to listen and watch. She had a curious fascination with things like wind and rain. Maybe she liked all nature, because she really liked the stars also, but here it was: the wind. All the boys were with the men, and Grandmom was busy with Aunt Nett. Ellie was quite happy to be alone, or almost alone. Lined up at the foot of her bed were Raggedy Ann, a cloth doll as tall as she was, and a Kewpie doll from Uncle Fay. (Those Merchant Marine trips created quite a homecoming, as everyone got something from a strange place in the world.) Also lined up like soldiers were the clothespin dolls with painted faces that Grandmom had made for Ellie to play with before the *real* dolls came into her life. All of the little painted faces had smiles—or what Ellie might at some times imagine as surprise—but they were faces.

Also stacked against the others were the spool dolls. They were made by a girl in the village named Eleanora who was too ill to leave her house, so nobody ever saw her, and she made these dolls from thread spools. They were strung together with twine, painted, and wore hats and clothes. They were really beautiful. Grandmom made sure Ellie had a few of those. These dolls were her friends, and she was not about to abandon those old toys in disrespect. The new dolls would just have to understand.

Sometimes the wind howled, but it was never steady. It came in gusts, some quiet, some more angry. Heavy bursts shook the house, and Ellie could hear it blow over the chairs on the porch below. The storm began to whistle through the boards and created squeaks. She thought that this wind had its own personality. She could barely remember what the others sounded like, because she was younger, but Ellie liked the wind. It felt and smelled good, and perhaps this one was just angry. She remembered trying to "see" the wind when they were coming home from school, but it had gone to make a mightier gust. Sometimes the wind would be gentle, but it never really stopped. She guessed it was just regrouping to get a better speed going. Once in a while it growled in a very low register. At times it rumbled into itself, resembling the faraway whine of a wounded animal. It sounded sort of like the wolves did, late at night when she listened, and she wished she could know what they were saying. A couple of times the wind would sing, then cry, and the tune was always lonely. The moans were sorrowful, then they grew very angry. The wind never heeded what was in its way. It either went through it or pushed it over—bounced off or tore down—on its quest to get *somewhere*.

The rain was coming in torrents, like sheets of solid blue bubbly curtains that were hard to see through. The wind and the rain were having a contest of which could be the noisiest. Ellie was fascinated. Just looking out the window was entertainment. She was not afraid. After a while Blake joined her, and they both stretched out on their bellies, across the bed, head in hands, propped up on their elbows and marveling at the sights and smells of the hurricane. Once in a while they'd utter an *oooohhhh* or an *aaaahhhh* when the wind was especially fierce. It had no conscience, seeming not to care if it tore up or took away something they liked. Too bad! It treated everything the same. Didn't it know the lighthouse was special?

But the lighthouse never moved. Sometimes they could hardly see it, yet it stayed right there—tolerating the limbs and small debris blowing by, even hitting it. The lighthouse was also a massive presence, and when up against the wind, the lighthouse was going to triumph.

The storm did come, and it tried, but in the end, not a single person packed up and left. As Grandpop always said, "You know? Everyone in this world has to deal with Mother Nature where they live. In Japan and China there are cyclones and earthquakes. In India, monsoons. In Europe it is harsh winters and blizzards, or volcanic eruptions. South

America: volcanic eruptions and earthquakes. Other places are plagued with drought, floods, tornadoes, and wildfires. I prefer the hurricane as my disaster of choice. The only people afraid of hurricanes are those who are not ready for them. That is not us."

Once the weather subsided, the islanders started to move around. They found that the roof had been blown off at Mr. O'Neal's house, so the men gathered together to make a plan to get it back on quickly. The kids in the village were running around saying that you could put your finger on Mr. O'Neal's couch and the water would shoot straight up. Some said three feet! Naturally Blake was bound to do that. And here he was, hanging around with Grandpop and the men, who were discussing the wood, where to get it, who would help . . . a perfect opportunity.

"Pssst, Ellie. Watch this." Blake poked his finger in the plush arm of the sofa, and the water shot up so fast it hit him right between the eyes. He jumped back stuttering and wiping his face. Ellie was holding her sides, and Luke hotfooted it over there to do it, too. As Grandpop turned around to see the ruckus, he got an eye full of Luke jamming his fist down in Mr. O'Neal's couch and spraying water all over himself and his cohorts.

"Get away from there!" Grandpop bellowed, and they hopped away like they were on fire.

Didn't anyone seem to care that poor Mr. O'Neal didn't have a decent sofa anymore? For the youngest villagers, it was all about bragging rights.

"I did it. . . ."

"So did I."

"But it hit the highest when I did it!"

The contest was just a part of being a kid.

———

Ellie had her recitation of "The Raggedy Man" practiced to perfection. It was a poem she learned from Grandpop. When she got her Raggedy Ann doll, Pop of course had a story to go with it. He remembered a poem he had read at an earlier time. It was a rather long one with many stanzas, which Grandpop felt might be too much for the talented little girl, so he wrote down a version he felt she could deliver with the flavor of the actual poem. She stood on one foot, then the other, to get the dialect correct, and when she made mistakes, it made the poem even more interesting. Her version was probably more entertaining than the original. Blake, on the other hand, would be doing a dance. He loved to dance, and when it was his turn, with Pop playing *Red Winged Blackbird*, on the harmonica, the lively tune prompted every single person, including Grandpop to get up and do the jig that Blake taught them.

> O the raggedy Man! He works fer Pa;
> An' he's the goodest man ever you saw!
> He comes to our house every day,
> An' waters the horses, an' feeds 'em hay;
> An' he opens the shed—an' we all ist laugh
> When he drives out our little old wobble-ly calf;
> An' nen—ef our hired girl says he can—
> He milks the cow fer 'Lizabuth Ann.—
> Ain't he a' awful good Raggedy Man?
> Raggedy! Raggedy! Raggedy Man!
>
> W'y, The Raggedy Man—he's ist so good,
> He splits the kindlin' an' chops the wood;
> An' nen he spades in our garden, too,
> An' does most things 'at *boys* can't do.—
> He climbed clean up in our big tree
> An' shooked a' apple down fer me—
> An' nother'n, too, fer 'Lizabuth Ann—
> An' nother'n, too, fer The Raggedy Man.—
> Ain't he a' awful kind Raggedy Man?
> Raggedy! Raggedy! Raggedy Man!

An' The Raggedy Man, he knows most rhymes,
    An' tells 'em, ef I be good, sometimes;
    Knows 'bout Giunts, an' Griffuns, an' Elves,
    An' the Squidgicum-Squees 'at swallers the'rselves;
    An', wite by the pump in our pasture-lot,
    He showed me the hole 'at the Wunks is got,
    'At lives 'way deep in the ground, an' can
    Turn into me, er 'Lizabuth Ann!
    Er Ma, er Pa, er The Raggedy Man!
        Ain't he a funny old Raggedy Man'?
            Raggedy! Raggedy! Raggedy Man!

The Raggedy Man—one time when he
Wuz makin' a little bow-'n'-orry fer me,
Says "When you're big like your Pa is,
Air *you* go' to keep a fine store like his—
An' be a rich merchant—an' wear fine clothes?—
Er what *air* you go' to be, goodness knows?"
An' nen he laughed at 'Lizabuth Ann,
An' I says "M go' to be a Raggedy Man!—
    I'm ist go' to be a nice Raggedy Man!"
            Raggedy! Raggedy! Raggedy Man!

The Find

When Luke and Ellie managed to coax Blake away from the "magic couch," they decided to go exploring.

"Grandpop," Ellie asked, "can we walk back home? We'll go by the back way down by where Mr. Rocky lives and cut across. We promise we won't go by the beach. Please, Grandpop, we'll be careful, and I'll bet we beat you home."

Grandpop agreed. He knew he would be needed to draw up the plans on O'Neal's roof and was discussing it with the other men. Captain Charlie was an excellent builder. He was so far the only college graduate on the island, and he had majored in architecture and engineering at what was then the Agricultural & Technical College of North Carolina, now known as North Carolina State, in Raleigh. So the locals deferred to him when it came to structures. He knew he would be there longer than he had planned, so taking into consideration that Luke was almost twelve, he thought that they could get in little danger on that back road. Luke had a level head. He was an academic and an athlete, and he did everything his grandfather could want. Yessir, Luke was Grandpop's man. This would be okay.

"All right, sweetheart. Go ahead. Mind Luke—and Luke, if she doesn't, you tell me, and both of you keep Blake out of trouble. Don't let him out of your sight. Don't go near any water, not sound ner sea. Stay on the path, don't stop and play. If you dilly-dally, you know somebody will tell me, and you won't be able to leave the yard for a month." (That wasn't a very big threat, since they never left the yard anyway, but it was all Grandpop could think of at such short notice.) "And for heaven's sake, keep your shoes on! Don't want you to be stepping on any nails or glass. Go on, straight home!" Then Grandpop turned back to help the others.

The kids took off down the road toward the footpath leading them to the lighthouse. This was more of a treat to them than most anything they could do. They liked to walk in the village. They didn't get to do that very often. They were always driving through or going straight to the lighthouse beach, directly away from the village. But here they were, smack in the middle, so of course they would pass through lots of strange sights on their way—the long way—around through the town in order to get home. They could see where everybody else lived and what they had. They marveled at the people who had fences, and there were unusual things in everybody's yard. The sandy two-track roads were adorned on both sides with wild rosebushes and flowers called phlox that clustered everywhere. The JoBell flower seemed to spring up wherever there was an empty space, making the vacant fields between houses look like a blanket of red. Butterflies were plentiful, as there was a lot to keep them busy. Ellie especially liked the colorful varieties of the beautiful flying fairies.

Some places near the edge of a wooded patch, there were blackberry bushes. The locals considered picking blackberries an island pastime, especially when they had to go into the woods to get them. The girls would take baskets with them and come back with so many that they had to make a pie or a cake. There were too many to just eat alone. Ellie liked them with the cream that Grandmom made from cow's milk. Twinkle, the cow, was quite happy to oblige, and Grandmom loved feeding Ellie milk. She wanted her to be strong. There was much to come. Grandmom always worried that Ellie would fall prey to the sickness that had taken Annie. She took great measures to ensure that this little girl ate correctly and got plenty of sleep.

As they passed the woods on the road leading to Mr. Rocky's house, they decided to take a little detour through the edge of the woods, just to kick up some old logs and maybe meet up with their wolves. Since the hurricane, they had not seen much of their wolves, and the children were a little worried about how they had weathered the storm. Nobody knew about the lighthouse wolves except Grandpop and Grandmom. Even Luke and Blake's parents, Bill and Nett, did not know about them. They knew they were there, but they didn't *know* about them. It was a secret the kids shared with their grandpop and grandmom Dessa, and that was enough.

The blood of the "knowing" passed through the Jennette line, both male and female. The male was a carrier but did not inherit the abilities. Only a female was able to demonstrate the skills that marked bestowal. The Jennette gifts were granted through an old Croatoan shaman, Odessa's ancestral grandmother. The endowment did not manifest itself with every generation, but throughout history, each female was gifted with a sixth sense of awareness. Only a few of the Jennette women exhibited the full set of powers. Odessa had the "knowing," but her daughter, Annie— Ellie's mother—was beginning to struggle with the powers. Odessa knew that Annie had more of the powers than she, as Annie "saw" the death of her husband at sea.

There were also other signs that Annie was gifted. She had the ability to see the future, for example, and she had an understanding of the animal world. Most surprising was her ability to "make things happen."

Annie also knew that she was different, and she was not comfortable with her talents. She was afraid of them. During those last days, when she and her mother spent so much time together, in her feverish state she revealed her torments to her mother, who understood. Odessa prayed for the strength to help her daughter, but it did not come.

Odessa had known from her mother that her own visions were a part of what the Jennette women referred to as the "knowing," and that it was natural in their family. Later in life, after she married Charlie Gray, Odessa dreamed that one of her female children would receive the full complement of powers, and that Odessa would then be elevated to help the child with them. Odessa knew that she, herself, would only be a guide to that child. When Jeanette was born, she kept a close watch, but nothing unusual appeared in the child. Then, when Iva was born, she thought maybe it was this girl, and that also did not materialize. From Annie's birth, she kept a close watch, and over time Odessa was convinced that this child was the one she envisioned in her dream. Annie proved not to be strong enough to control or cope with the special talents, and she became more and more ill.

Odessa had told Charlie before their marriage about the blessings, and years later she explained about the dream. It was their secret. The knowledge was hard for Charlie to wrap his mind around, but he knew from the beginning that the Jennette women were special, and he was willing to join with the family because of his love for Odessa. Together they would handle whatever came. When Joseph insisted he could take care of his beautiful Annie, he was also made aware of her special gifts. He and Captain Charlie had many late-night discussions on the subject, and both felt honored to be part of such a history.

When Joseph died, Captain Charlie and Odessa saw the sharp decline in Annie—in her health, mind, and will to live. They prepared for the loss of their troubled daughter and were hopeful that the birth of the child would bring her back. That did not happen. Because they knew the gifts only manifested themselves once in several generations, they did not expect their little Ellie to be any more affected than either Jennette or Iva. But eventually Odessa began to notice the uniqueness in Ellie, and she

THE FIND ★ 47

realized that Ellie was the child in the dream. She knew, and through her, Charlie knew. As Ellie showed signs of her mental awareness, her grandmother tried not to encourage or foster the gifts. She thought Ellie was too young. Looking back, Odessa wondered if she had made mistakes with Annie, vowing not to repeat them with Ellie.

They were not surprised when the wolves returned. They knew them to be a part of all of this, a protective part. Neither Charlie nor Odessa objected to the presence of the wolves. It would be up to Ellie to handle them, and they knew she could.

As the children played around near the woods on their way home, they came upon places at the edge of the ridge that had dropped off when the tide ate into the core of the hill leading down to the sound, making the embankment steeper than before. They were near the back of Miss Lilly's house. Miss Lilly was one of Jeanette's best friends, so they were comfortable to be in that area and felt safe not actually sticking to the path as Grandpop had said. Miss Lilly did not have any children, and if they were lucky she would see them out the kitchen window and invite them in for cookies or fudge. Miss Lilly was a baker. She provided the very best treats at all the church functions and was always looking for someone who could try out one of her new recipes. But Miss Lilly was in her yard, doing damage control from the heavy tide that had spoiled some of her garden. She only raised a hand in acknowledgment of the youngsters and went on with her business, under that ridiculously huge yellow hat that shielded her from the sun—except that she lived in the woods, and there wasn't any sun. Seemed to the kids that the hat might be the reason she wasn't married.

So they meandered along, goofing around, cookieless. As they drew near the low part of the wooded ridge, Luke saw something shiny down near the bank of the sound.

"Hey . . . look. What's that?" Luke pointed to the shiny object winking at them from the mud near the edge of the water.

"Better not go down there" warned Ellie. "Grandpop said no going near the water!" she chided in a singsongy voice.

"But look, it might be gold!" Luke answered, paying no attention to what Ellie was saying.

"Ain't no gold 'round here. Probably just a piece of glass, and Grandpop said don't go near the water!" Ellie repeated.

Luke glanced back at her in acknowledgment and gave a half-cocked smile. He was just too curious, so he picked his way through the dry marsh grass until he was near the edge of the water line and sat down on a fallen log to take off his shoes. He was determined to get that thing that the tide had uncovered, and if he didn't get his shoes wet, nobody would know he was near the water. He needed to be close, but not so close that he would tip over and fall in. He reasoned in his head that probably even Grandpop would be interested in something shiny that the storm had washed out of its grave. Carefully leaning over, he reached down and grabbed hold of what looked like a glistening stick. He was persistent, and by the time he got the whole thing out of the muddy bank, Blake and Ellie were right down there with him. Nobody mentioned anything about what Grandpop said. They were all caught up in this wonderful find. They stared at the old sword Luke had pulled out of the mud. The handle looked like a cuff. They had never seen such a piece.

"Oh, my!" said Ellie.

Luke was stupefied. He didn't say a word, but he just kept washing off the mud from the precious find and admiring what he had.

"I'm keeping it!" he announced emphatically and, with a look of utter wonderment, kept turning it over and over, looking at it.

"If you do, Grandpop will know where we were," Blake said. "I wasn't gonna tell, but Grandpop will know we were near the water, and he said not to."

This was a problem. Luke wanted that sword mighty badly, but he also didn't want to lose his grandfather's trust. Luke had to think this one out.

The three adventurers began to make their way back to the pine-covered path, Luke holding on to the cuff of the handle and dragging that sword behind him, careful not to touch the blade lest it be sharper than it looked. He knew he would have to explain a cut.

Everybody decided not to say a word about the find. They talked and talked about it on the way home. It was old—really old—and they wanted to tell but they just couldn't, so they decided to hide it in the barn until a better plan came to mind. But happy? You bet they were. What a wonderful story they had, and they couldn't tell anyone!

On the way back home, the children got into as much trouble as they dared. Luke was cutting down reeds and underbrush, all of them pretending they were in the jungle, hacking their way to safety, trying to get away from the lions. Luke was careful not to swing the sword close to either Ellie or Blake, and also careful not to let them have a go at chopping. They were too young, he said, as they continued to beg. After a while they concentrated on their adventure and stopped asking to "help clear the way."

Nearing the house they could tell that Grandpop was home, and they hoped they were not in trouble. They knew that they had taken longer than they were supposed to, so they were cautious not to call attention to themselves.

They decided, though, that the next chance they got, they were going back to see if they could find anything else. What if this was a pirate's sword, and there was a treasure chest in the mud? No telling what kinds of things the tide had uncovered. It looked like the water had come up quite a bit where they found the sword, and maybe there was another one, maybe something better—or maybe Blackbeard himself had washed up there. Yessirree, they were going back!

Luke, Ellie, and Blake crept toward the back of the barn and looked around. They needed to get in the barn without anyone seeing them and without spooking the horses. They played in the barn with the horses a lot, even fed them sometimes, and were always giving them carrots. They even gave them apples when they had them, but that was rare, and then it was only a piece. The horses had learned to have a soft mouth with the kids. They were used to their smell and knew to be careful not to snap or bite. But they did whinny a little and snort a few times when their friends entered. That was their way of asking for a treat. They always got something special when the kids came around, even if it was just a friendly rub.

Luke began to look around to find the right hiding place for the sword.

"Here is the perfect place," said Blake. "This old chest under all the blankets we use for the horses' back."

"Yeah, that would be great—to have Grandpop or Uncle Jack cut their hand when they reach in to grab one for riding. Nope, keep looking," said Ellie.

"How about here?" Blake kicked over a pile of old boxes that were left over from the equipment and new tools Grandpop just received from the government. The wooden crates were long, emptied of the telescopes that had been in them. The tools for fixing the lenses of the Hatteras light were already up on the top floor of the beacon, ready to be used. Grandpop was a bit of a packrat and never really threw away anything that could be used later, especially wooden packing crates. They were rare and could come in handy for lots of things.

"Great job, Blake. These are perfect, and if we put it in the long one on the bottom, it will be a long time before he decides to use that one," said Luke. The plan was hatched. Luke pried open one of the wooden crates and put in the sword.

"Perfect! Just fits, but you know," Luke said quietly, "we never keep anything from Grandpop, and he never keeps anything from us."

"Grandmom's gonna know," said Blake. "You know she will. Grandmom knows everything."

"We have to tell, but let's wait 'til he gets in a good mood, like when we are all in the jalopy, going somewhere, so he doesn't cuff me on the back of the head."

"Well, I don't want to be the one cuffed!" said Blake. "He won't smack Ellie. He's always careful with her, cause she's a girrrrllll," he said, dragging out the word to get under Ellie's skin—and it worked. She started chasing him around the barn and caught him near one of the stalls. She wrestled him to the ground in the soft straw, tickling him 'til he squealed. Then they heard Grandpop yelling.

"You young-uns better not get those horses riled up, or I'll be in there to crack some skulls."

Of course, Grandpop's bark was bigger than his bite, but they all had experienced a dose of a whipping from Grandpop, and they did not want another one. Pop's style was to make them pick their own switch. That proved to be a problem. If you picked a skinny one, it would sting your legs. If you picked a thicker one, he would whack you on the butt, and that was maybe worse. There was no winning with the switch thing. They learned it was best not to get a switching in the first place. The only solution was to avoid the punishment by being just as good as they could figure, yet still be bad when it was absolutely necessary. These three had gotten good at that.

★ 7 ★

The Wolves

That night, all three were in the main keeper's quarters. Luke and Blake were to spend the night with Ellie. Bill and Nett had gone into the village to a gathering at Tommy's house and knew it would be late when they returned, so Grandpop and Grandmom agreed to keep the children while their parents were off to join their friends. This was the perfect time to tell Grandpop, but Luke wasn't ready. Instead, he decided to inquire about the wolves. So when Grandpop started to tell one of his deer stories, Luke interrupted him with a little side story of his own.

"Grandpop, how come we have wolves and nobody's supposed to know about them? And where did they come from? And how come Daddy and Momma don't know about them, and where do they go when they are not around us, and—?"

"Whoa there, partner," said Grandpop. "Where did all that come from? Was it the storm you were worried about? 'Cause they are surely okay."

"No," chimed in Blake. "We talk about it all the time, and just wondered why they are special to us and nobody else? All the other people are scared of them."

"Don't worry, Pop. We like them, and they like us," said Ellie.

"But nobody ever told me about *why* the wolves like us. They just tell me that I should be glad," said Blake. "I am glad, Grandpop. I am."

"Looks like this is going to be a doozy of a story tonight." Grandpop glanced at Odessa, and she half smiled—as the children had asked the wrong person—but Charlie could get into it enough to allow these special souls to begin digesting their uniqueness. She gave Charlie a *knowing* look, and he continued, "'Dessa, got any of that chocolate cake left? We might be here for a while."

Odessa got up with a sly smile still playing across her face. This was going to be her story, and she didn't want to miss the telling of it. She hurried to the back of the house where the kitchen and side porches were and pulled out the cake from the area where all the food was kept. She cut one big slice and three medium slices, put them on plates, and returned to the living room where Grandpop sat with Ellie on his lap and one boy on either side. She made smaller pieces because she didn't want the sugar to keep the kids awake all night, and a larger one because she knew Charlie was going to need the energy for this one.

Grandpop began. "Luke, do you remember the story of Ellie's birth?"

"Yes, Pop," said Luke, "but I don't think you ever told Blake."

"I know, son, and I think he is old enough to understand now, don't you?"

Before Luke could answer, Blake broke in. "I am, Pop. I am. Tell me, too."

"Well," Grandpop started again, this time more slowly, as he intended to choose his words carefully. Ellie leaned forward, as did Luke. They had always been fascinated with how their family seemed to be different from anyone else they knew. Maybe all families had spirits and wolves, and they also did not talk about it. But these two could keep a secret, and this one was the most special of all. They were actually glad that Blake was old enough for the story. Secrets are best when shared.

Grandpop explained, "Ellie was born on September seventeenth during the full moon, the one that everyone calls the harvest moon. They call it that because it is larger than the other full moons that come on the monthly cycle, and it allows the farmer to work for a longer period of daylight to gather his crops. It is lower in the sky, and as you all have seen and talked about, over the years it also appears to be twice as big."

Ellie was thinking then of how she looked out her bedroom window, knowing it was her moon, and how she always wished on it. Most all of her wishes came true. The wishes were never complicated, as she was a happy little girl who had most of what she knew was out there to have. On this island, her family was as well off as most, and Ellie was not cursed with envy. She did not look at others and wish for what they had. She waited all year for her birthday moon. Birthdays were joyful times with the Gray clan. All the children gleefully anticipated celebrations. Ellie got just as excited when it was Luke's or Blake's birthday as she did for her own. Luke was born under the beaver moon, in November, when animals begin to build shelters or look for a place to spend the winter. Blake was born under the snow moon, in February, usually the coldest month.

Grandpop was still talking. "On the night of the birth, we took our daughter Annie, Ellie's mom, to a place in Hatteras Village, the building where the Weather Bureau is located now. But then, that building was used for several things, one being a hospital, with a room where medicines were kept. The back room was equipped with several necessary things for keeping a patient comfortable while they waited to go away to Elizabeth City, the nearest hospital.

"We called in two ladies who had experience with the sick to meet us there. These people were said also to be gifted in local cures of this old island. We knew who these caregivers were. Their knowledge was passed down to them from medicine men and women who recognized their talent. They used herbs that grew on the island and made remedies for healing. Certain muds, grasses, and plants—when boiled or brewed together—heal cuts, bites, fevers, and other illnesses that plague humans. Here on the island, away from professional doctors, we needed these concoctions, ointments, and wraps to draw out discomforts.

"You know that when you get a bee sting, I put tobacco in my mouth and chew, then mix it with fat from an animal, and put it on your wound to draw out the poison. The juices in my saliva combine with the leaf of the tobacco and the fat to create a poultice. Sometimes, Ellie, when you are sick, I put a salve on your chest to draw out the poison. That patch is called a poultice. I learned that from my grandmother, who learned it from her grandmother. The Indians had a shaman—a doctor—who performed healing on stricken tribesmen. This is knowledge we learned from them. All of our communities have someone who knows the healing powers of natural plants, and how to brew or mix them to counteract an ailment. It is necessary for these things to be studied, so most people on this island know who to go to when they are in need of healing.

"This woman, Miss Bertie, was one your grandmom and mother call a midwife, or someone who is especially skilled in helping a young woman deliver a child. Most babies on the island were born at home, with the help of the midwife or helper in attendance, but our Annie was very sick. She was born with the same affliction as your grandmother Odessa. It's an unusual blood condition. A child born with this is especially susceptible to long illnesses, when other people with simple ailments simply shake them off with no ill effects. Annie, Ellie's mother, was just such a child. Therefore, we thought Ellie would be a frail child, as frail as her mother. Grandmother, also born with the disorder, does not seem to be bothered with severe symptoms. However, over time, Ellie has proven not to be as affected as was her mother, Annie.

"When her husband, Joseph—Ellie's father—drowned a few months before Ellie was born, Annie never fully recovered from the depression that came with the loss. Joseph was probably the only person in the world, except for your grandmother and me, whom Annie trusted to understand her condition, and around whom she laughed and was like a normal girl. So, when Joseph left her, even though she was going to bear a child and have it for comfort, it did not seem to matter. She had lost her best friend, and she couldn't or wouldn't get over it. She never got out of bed after he passed on. She just willed herself to die and be with him. She did not think that she could ever raise a child, because she knew she was weak. We knew this was going to be a sad time, so when she showed signs of the child coming, we took her to Hatteras, where all the medical supplies were located. There was also a special ham radio with the capability to communicate back and forth across the sound to the nearest hospital. This time it was set up to talk to a real doctor, so Miss Bertie from Buxton—and Miss Rita, another local healer from Kinnakeet Village—were brought in to help Annie deliver her child. They did the best they could.

"Now, your grandmom and I are very spiritual people—and we hope you are, too—so we went in another room, got on our knees, and prayed for God, His Son, Jesus, and all the saints of heaven to help our beautiful child live to have this baby. They say that when Ellie was born, Annie took her last breath. But something the old people know to have happen did happen: Annie's spirit left her body with her last breath, but at that time, another breath was taking over. Her daughter began to breathe.

"At the time of Ellie's first cry, the room was bathed in a silvery light, and a silver blue cloud hovered over the hospital bed. Now, in the Bible, it is written that sometimes people have been visited by 'angels of the Lord,' and we think that Ellie was visited by an angel of the Lord. We think this angel decided at that moment that she would take the place of Ellie's mother and watch over Ellie as her mother would have if she had lived. The Bible talks in the Old Testament about angels—and some people believe, and some don't. I don't know which one of those I am. You know, we don't go to the Pentecostal church, they believe a little stronger."

"Miss Lucy does," said Luke. "They say she sometimes talks funny when she is in church, the boys told me."

"Well, your grandmother and I are friends with all the villagers—the ones who go to the Methodist church like we do, and the ones who go to the Pentecostal church, like you say Miss Lucy does. Everybody has the right to worship where they want. We don't make any judgments about that, and you shouldn't either. When you get older, you will decide what you think about God and his son, Jesus, but for the time being, we are raising you like we were raised, and that is good enough for now."

Grandpop was careful always to let the children find their own way. He considered himself a guide, and he firmly believed that Ellie was special and had special spirits looking after her, because she came into this world without parents or guides. It was hard enough with guides, but a child who at some point may think she is different might need someone close enough to explain the mysteries to her. And Ellie was not going to be that child who wondered. As Grandpop reflected, Ellie had adjusted quite well being with him and Odessa, especially with Jeanette and Bill around all the time. What had started out as being troublesome and uncomfortable had proven to be the opposite. Ellie had developed the toughness of any other little girl, maybe because Luke and Blake never let her get away with feeling sorry for herself. They actually thought they were all the same, one just as loved and cared for as the next. When the chips were down, it was always three against the world.

"Do I have a spirit watching over me, too?" asked Blake.

"We all do, son. We are never alone. Sometimes when you think inside, *This is right* or *This is wrong*, it is your guiding spirit trying to make sure you choose the correct path."

Captain Charlie looked at his wife, feeling that it was comforting to create a sense of reassurance among the children—to set their minds at ease that they were always going to be taken care of. This was especially true with Ellie. She should never think that she was alone with no one to look after her.

Grandpop continued his story. "Miss Bertie and Miss Rita sent your grandmother and me home. 'Nothin' you can do now,' Miss Bertie said. 'Go on home. We will send out to some of the new mothers we know in the village to get milk for the child, and we'll watch over her 'til we think she is strong enough to be sent back home so's you both can take care of her. If you need help after you get home, Rita and I will be right there. Just come get us. Your daughter Nett has a little boy, so she knows and she can help. Now don't you folks worry. This baby is going to be fine.'

"With that, Grandmom and I got in the wagon and came home. We didn't have a car then—it was horses and the wagon—but our horses were big ones, and even though it was night, we knew they would find the way.

"We started for home in silence, hoping and saying prayers that our baby would continue to breathe. Hoping that the silver and blue light would stay around. It was a hard and heavy wait. A couple of days later the phone rang: our signal, one long and three short rings, in the keeper's office. It was the Coast Guard station. They told us they had been contacted by the ladies at the government building taking care of Ellie, and our little baby was ready to come home. We were so excited and a little scared. We had not had a baby to care for since your uncle Jack, but we did have a little experience with Luke, and your mom declared she would help. She acted like it was going to be her baby. The whole family was ready to see this little girl who had been born under the special light.

"We quickly hitched up the wagon and horses and headed to Hatteras to pick up Ellie. Grandmom took with her the white wicker basket she and Annie had fitted out with soft material during the long time that Annie was in bed. Grandmom had hoped that a little sewing and preparation and happy conversation would help Annie feel better. The basket was covered in handmade lace and embroidered silk that they both spent long hours stitching, and lined with both silk and satin that they ordered through the Sears & Roebuck catalog, all soft blankets to cushion the sides of the basket, which would serve to be the infant's first bed."

Remembering the hours of love that went into that basket made Odessa's heart heavy with the loss of her daughter.

"The waning harvest moon was still bright enough to light the way, and the roads were solid. There had been a slight rain, and it packed them down pretty hard. We found our path firm enough that we wouldn't have to go over to the hard sand of the beach wash but could go the whole way on the two-track road running down the middle on the land side of the dunes. When we got there, Miss Bertie had wrapped Ellie up tightly so that she wouldn't get a chill in the open wagon.

"As they were putting the small bundle in the basket, Miss Rita leaned over and whispered in Grandmom's ear, 'She has the condition, "the royal disease," you know, but Miss Odessa, I heard 'bout your family. This one looks strong as a bear. It seems to react better on her. She don't seem to be sickly.'

"Then she leaned back and gave a knowing wink and looked away." Captain Charlie was recalling the night in such detail that his eyes looked wet.

"Grandmom had nodded in acknowledgment to Miss Rita, leaned down and sniffed the baby, and said to me in a soft voice, 'We'll handle all this one at a time. Right now, she's fine, and we intend she will stay that way.'

"It was dark when we started back to Buxton, through the Frisco Woods. We got in the thick of it, and the horses came to a sudden stop. In the road, a pack of wolves appeared in front of the wagon, blocking the way. The horses stood still, frost coming out of their snorting nostrils, and they lightly, not deeply, pawed the ground. They looked eye to eye with the two large leaders of the pack. The wolves so far were peaceful, their yellow eyes staring at us intensely but not showing signs of anger or hostility. I was frozen in my mind and powerless to move. It was such a shock. Here we were, in the famous Frisco Woods, where wolves had been known to live for years, and there they were.

"They were majestic looking. One of them looked directly at me, head cocked, studying my face. Their fur was a dusty tan color, with white and caramel specks around the mane and neck and a really dark ring around the eyes. Their eyes slanted downward toward their nose, and the fur around the muzzle was pure white. One wolf, the one right in front, was almost white, with reddish specks. Two of them, the first two, held their tails high, an indication of dominance. The others just stared, not moving, tails relaxed. One of them, smaller, was almost black, with white tips of fur on the ears, and around his eyes, the rest of the fur was totally black. It was striking.

"The largest threw its head back, mouth rounded for sound, eyes closed, ears back, only bottom teeth slightly visible. It looked up at the waning moon and howled. The others followed suit—all in their own individual pitch, as each had a unique sound, with the pups yodeling out their puppy howls to match the mood. The sound filled the woods. It was one long howl, and then it stopped. The silence was just as deafening as the howling had been. There were several of them, maybe six adults and four small pups. The two larger wolves had long legs and carried themselves as the leaders of the pack.

"I looked at Odessa and saw on her face a look I had never seen before and have not seen since. She was calm. She had a 'knowing,' something beyond any words. The horses were calm—it is unusual for horses to be calm around wolves—and I knew at that moment that the stories I had heard about your grandmother's family were true. Your grandmom is part of a direct line of the English settlers who came to this island to escape the unfriendly Indians of the mainland. They were known to have intermarried with the Croatoan Indian tribe who took them in. Grandmom has, I guess, as much Indian blood as anyone on this island.

"She is a descendant of a line of people, protected by the shamans of the earliest Indians. Her ancestral grandmother was the daughter of the greatest shaman in our Indian lore. She was Manteo's mother, Weroansqua. Weroansqua's daughter had a girl, Kweepi, who married an Englishman, Jenet, later spelled Jennette. His parents came to the island when the child Virginia Dare was brought here to escape the Roanoke

Indians. The child was the pride of the Croatoan tribe. She had light hair and eyes. They had not seen a little girl like this. It was as if she was exceptional and blessed by nature. She was pampered and honored by their medicine men and assigned a protector, a white wolf.

"As I watched in wonder at the horses—realizing that they were not nervous and knowing that they are instinctively anxious around wolves—this sight of them actually waiting was unbelievable. As if all of this was not enough to give me a heart attack, Odessa just sat there with her cheek on Ellie's, eyes half closed. They looked so peaceful. This feeling was broken by something even stranger. The largest wolf, who was lighter than the others, jumped on the bed of the wagon and slowly moved toward Grandmom and Ellie. It was the female, and her golden eyes had blue specks at the top. I will never forget those eyes. They say if you ever look into the eyes of a wolf your life is changed forever. I believe that. They were kind eyes, but I knew they could narrow to look fierce if the situation called for it. The huge wolf lowered her head near the head of the baby, and as I am watching, hardly breathing, Grandmom lifts our precious grandbaby toward the wolf. The creature nuzzles the child and licks its cheek, sniffs all around the bundle, as wolves are known to 'follow the blood,' and this quickened my heart. But then the massive animal turns and, with light steps, jumps off the wagon bed."

"What's 'nuzzle'?" asked Blake.

"Best I can say is that she puts her nose on the baby's cheek and sniffs her several times, smelling her like she would if it were a wolf child," said Grandpop, a lump in his throat and tears welling up in his big blue eyes. He continued, "When the wolf licked Ellie, I held my breath. I was still afraid—after all I am not of that clan, I didn't know inside myself what Grandmom knows. This was all strange to me, too. When the mother wolf got to the ground, she stood in front of the horses. Her mate—large, but not as large as the female—also took his place in front of the horses.

"What happened next will stay with me forever. Both those wild creatures dropped to the ground, crouched flat, magnificent heads between their paws, looking up at the child, ears erect, but piercing eyes, shining in quiet reverence. At that point every wolf in the pack took the same stance, all but the pups, who crouched down on all fours, little heads down, and lay flat on the ground looking at their elders, not knowing yet, but with a feeling of something different. Still the horses did not move. Did they know something I did not know? I will never forget it. In a flash, the wolves parted the way and were gone. And children, I mean a flash. Against that crescent moon, a blue cloud with silver running through it swirled around the wagon. It was so bright I had to close my eyes."

"What was it, Grandpop?" asked Blake.

"Well, son, I think it was Ellie's spirit guide. I think she was there to let us have the feeling that everything was going to be all right. And, son, I think this aura—or unseen color that surrounds Ellie—is why she is picked on by the other girls. I think there is something about her that is unusual, and other children sense it when they are in her presence."

"Do I have it, too?" asked Blake.

"Blake, will you stop it and let Grandpop finish his story? You keep interrupting, and we will never get to your part if you don't shut up!" said Luke.

"But I want to know," Blake said under his breath, hardly moving his lips.

"Luke, don't talk to your brother like that. You know the story, and he doesn't! Be patient with him." Grandpop knew his youngest grandchild would be full of questions, and he was ready with answers.

To Blake, Grandpop said, "We'll get to your part, honey. It is just a longer bedtime story than I had counted on.

"I motioned for the horses to move forward, and as casually as they could, as big as they are, they slowly started walking, then trotting home. As we got closer to Buxton, the lighthouse was shining the way. I kept glancing back, but the pack of wolves had disappeared. Grandmom kissed Ellie's cheek just where the wolf had licked her, and we looked at each other, and there was a *knowing*.

"It was the first time since I courted your grandmom that I recalled the stories of your grandmother's family. I knew that her ancestors had come to the island from the mainland, ragged and afraid, as they had escaped the hostile Indians on Roanoke Island. There has always been a lot of folklore surrounding some of the families on the island, and your grandmother's family, the Jennettes, are one of them. We have always known the story of the settlers, the Indians, and the wolves. We knew not to mess with the wolves of Frisco. They were special. They lived in harmony with the Indians. In modern times we heard tell of the white wolf who looked out over the first English child, and it has been 300 years since anybody has seen a white.

"We know it is bad luck to kill a wolf, and we always thought of them as good luck because our wolves keep to the woods. They don't bother anybody, don't kill chickens, cattle, or dogs. I do not tell this to others. I keep it special between me and Odessa, and of course you, my babies. Know this: It isn't anything you should talk about. Sometimes I even wonder if I've seen what I've seen, but it is between us, and if you need to talk about anything or ask questions, you ask me or your grandmother. And Blake—yes, you and Luke have special spirits that protect you, too, and when it needs to, that spirit will light your way also."

"Pop, does mine have to be a girl? Could mine be a boy?" questioned Blake.

"Oh, son, I think it is whatever you feel it to be. It is in your heart. If you would rather talk to a boy, then that's okay, too. They are spirits, not human bodies. It is a feeling inside. Just not for me to say," said Grandpop. "But I will say that the angels appearing in both the Old and New Testaments of the Bible were referred to as taking the human form of a man."

Blake settled back with a sigh, satisfied, a slightly one-sided smile sneaking across his face.

What a kid, Captain Charlie thought. *Makes me smile even when I am sad.*

"Grandpop, we see the wolves sometimes," said Luke. "They seem to be watching us from behind the lighthouse, over in the woods, but they don't come out, and there are only three."

"Yes, son, there are three that you see. The rest of the pack stays hidden. There is one for each of you, and when you need them, they will be there. They will always be there. They are pack animals, and you are part of their pack. They never leave one of their pack behind. They take care of their sick, even if it means hunting for it and feeding it like they do their pups. I heard tell of a wolf that broke his jaw after being kicked in the head by a huge buck. He could not eat. The other wolves hunted, brought back food, chewed it up, and spit it into the old wolf's mouth so that he wouldn't starve to death."

"*Eeeeewwwww*," said Ellie, holding her hand over her mouth and nose. "That's nasty!"

"That's how they feed their pups. That's how birds feed their young also," Grandpop said, "and that's how they would feed you if you were ever in a bad spot and couldn't feed yourself. They protect their own, and you children are considered 'their own' to these wolves. They stay in the woods so that they can be close by. Usually they are in the shadows. You might catch a glimpse of them as they dart between the trees like fleeting dark clouds, but they don't show themselves. Mostly they are nocturnal."

"What's 'nocturnal'?" Blake fired off a defiant look at Luke, waiting for him to snap at him. Better not! Grandpop would smite him.

"It means they usually come out at night," said Grandpop. "They are not playful like a dog. They do not need you. They think you need them. They have a range of protective territory of about fifty miles, which takes up most of this island. They can smell their prey at least ten miles away and pick up sound at two miles away. Their territory, if it is the same as when the Indians were around, is near the Buxton and Frisco Woods.

Those woods used to be one huge wooded area, 'til the houses came. But Buxton Woods, closest to the hills near Mr. Rocky's, is native to the Croatoan, and probably most familiar to our wolfpack."

The three each shot a glance at the others, and all were thinking, *Could the wolves have been watching us today when we were in the woods?*

Blue and Silver Glow

 back at school, Luke was just beginning to experience what every kid aspired to. He was now entering the seventh grade and had moved into "the room." Built by the islanders, the school was a huge, long saltbox structure, resembling a lodge, with very high ceilings as a result of the roof's high-pitched style. It was divided into three areas across the length. On either side was a door leading into that section. The left section was the high school rooms with the cafeteria in the very back. The right side was the elementary classrooms, and in back, the restrooms. In the middle of the rectangle was an auditorium. Across the front of the building were huge windows high up, reaching the top. The same windows ran along each side and across the back. Having little electricity other than a generator, the school needed light—and in the spring and fall, air—from the heat of the season. Its position in the clearing, on high ground and surrounded by tall pine trees on three sides, prevented the frequent storms from damaging the structure.

The back lot sloped down the hill quite a ways, with a large area of flat land eventually leading to one of the many springs that ran like veins throughout the island. That back lot was the scene of many contests, especially the softball games that were played every day that weather permitted. Teams were chosen each week, using the hand-over-hand bat method. In the back stretching between the rest rooms and the cafeteria was a long porch, with doors leading into all areas that were opened from the porch. The long steps across the back porch was where students used to hang out. Everybody watched softball games from those porch steps.

There were three classrooms on the elementary side. The first room was where the first, second, and third grades studied. The middle room housed grades four, five, and six. Then there was *the room*, where the older children were taught, grades seven and eight. To most of the children, this was the magic room. Everything exciting happened there. They had visitors who came to talk to them about special subjects. A popular vocation to aspire to was piloting a boat. These were the days of local men piloting vessels through the tricky shoals of the Pamlico Sound, and those men were in great demand, so that was a popular subject. Also, they heard about traveling the world with the Coast Guard, or skills like boatbuilding or net making. (The students actually got to go outside for net making, and it wasn't even recess.) Sometimes Captain Charlie was the speaker for the Lighthouse Service. Of course, regular studies were carried on, but by that time the children were old enough to know how to handle themselves, supposedly. When the teacher lost control, the parents took over. It seemed there were boyfriend-and-girlfriend situations in that room. It was the room to be looked forward to and respected.

Luke entered into this room a shy boy, and he quite expected he would have to prove himself at some time. But with a smile in his heart, he knew he could. His dad, Bill, had seen to that. When Bill was regular navy, he was a boxer. Quite a good one they say, and now he was teaching Jack and Lindy how to box. There were matches every Saturday night on the mainland, in Nags Head, at a place called the Casino. Bill had set up a boxing ring in the vacant side of the assistant keeper's quarters, and Lindy, Jack, and their friends took instruction from Bill on how to box. They had all of the proper equipment. Bill had bought it back from his training in the navy, and the Coast Guard provided the rest. It was fun to watch all the older boys sparring with each other and the seamen from the Coast Guard. There was also a punching speed bag and a heavy bag. Lindy was the bigger of the two, but Jack was quicker. They were all training to go to the Golden Gloves trials in Texas. Luke and Blake were allowed to spar once in a while with the guys, because the men wanted them to be able to take care of themselves.

Luke looked around and marveled at the growth spurt some of his classmates had experienced over the summer. The girls were prettier and more particular about their clothes and hair. If their hair did not look good enough for school, they wore a scarf all day. *How silly*, Luke thought. One girl wore a scarf every day. Did she have hair? It was a thing to contemplate if you finished your work early and had nothing else to think about. The boys had gained a little muscle, sometimes because they were now helping their fathers with pulling nets, building boats, or hauling freight. Everything took on a new look from last year, and it was only three months since. But Uncle Jack had educated Luke about the seventh grade before he left for another year of college. Luke was prepared.

This was also the first time Ellie, Blake, and Luke were all in separate rooms. Blake was glad about that. He didn't like that the two older kids had something to laugh about when it took place in their room, and he was not there to see it. Like the time Judy B, a girl from Frisco, asked Miss Mary if she could go to the bathroom. The teacher refused and told Judy B to finish her work, then turned to the children in the last two rows. The grades were sectioned off by rows, and as Miss Mary was dealing with one of the other grades, she therefore mistakenly ignored the request. A very mischievous child, Judy B was one of the girls who always wore a scarf, sometimes with pin curls still tightly wound under it. (Now, what was she waiting for with those pin curls? If you don't care how you look among your friends, who are you saving your pretty [?] hair for? The bus ride home? Such a strange girl.) Anyway, Judy B looked around and giggled to a couple of girls next to her, indicating that she wanted to borrow their scarves. It was a scarf world. Miss Mary's still had her attention on the other two rows.

The girls cupped their hands over their mouths to keep from laughing out loud, and with muffled sounds they reached in their pockets and handed over their two scarves to Judy B. Still, this was only observed by three people: Judy B and the two girls on either side of her desk. Everybody else was trying to finish their seat work, in anticipation of Miss Mary giving book work to the last two rows and coming back to start all over with the grade at the left of the room. Wow, if the boys had known what was going to happen, this would have been a better story.

Judy B snuck up to the front of the room and picked up the trash can. What kind of teacher would not know that happened? Miss Mary, whose behind-her-back name was "Bugtths Bunny"—that's what kind. Miss Mary was from Little Washington, a town across the Albemarle Sound south on the mainland. She was single, kinda old looking, maybe thirty, and just didn't know what she was getting into. She probably was assigned a teaching position by the state, as they did try to supply educational needs to the outlying areas, but she was not ready for this. Frumpy, funny-dressed Miss Mary—big ol' gap between her two front teeth, those two being a little bigger than the rest—couldn't control her volume and was busy spitting all over the sixth grade.

Judy B put the trash can under the top of her desk where her feet usually rested. She anchored the three scarves around the sides of the desktop with books and rulers holding them in place. (Judy B had every right to cover her hair with her scarf. It was a mess! Did the girl have a comb at home?) And behind those scarves, Judy B peed in that trash can. The noise of water hitting the papers and sides of the metal can awakened the whole room. There was so much commotion, laughter, kicking of feet, boys making trouble that poor Miss Mary was not exactly aware of where it was all coming from—until she spied the defiled trash can in the middle of the aisle and all the kids jumping out of their seats to get away from it . . . including Judy B, who was pointing and laughing the most.

Well, Miss Mary was so frustrated, she could not control the chaos taking place all over the room. She did not want to touch the can, and the children would not help her. They couldn't. They were all lining the walls of the room, holding their sides, not paying any attention to Miss Mary's screeching. One boy, Georgie Tolsen, jumped out of the window—which was not unusual for him. He did that at will. Because he was so mean, he just knew it was eventually going to be blamed on him. So he was outta there! Miss Mary started crying and ran out of the room, slamming the door until the windows rattled. The room went nuts! For the rest of the afternoon, it was game time. Finally the noise reached such a pitch that Mr. Austin, the principal, came to the door.

Between snorts of laughter, the youngsters gladly tattled on Judy B, who looked sheepishly around with eyes that said, "Don't let me get you alone on the playground. I'll whip your butt." Thing about it was, she could do it, and she was only in the fifth grade. Everybody was sent to the cafeteria, located on the high school side, to sit quietly while the cafeteria ladies stood guard, and Mr. Midgett, the janitor, was left to deal with the nasty trash can. Luke and Ellie imagined he must have thrown it away, because the next day, there was a different can.

Walking back to the lighthouse from school, Luke and Ellie tried to tell Blake about Judy B, but they could not stop laughing long enough for Blake to get the whole story. It was totally unfair that they shared a room and he was stuck in the first/second/third–grade room. When Luke got to move up to another room, it meant they were all in separate rooms, and that made Blake happy. His stories of the day became just as important as the other stories.

Concentration was important with three grades in a room. It was something a kid on the island learned early. The teacher in the first/second/
third–grade room assigned lots of classwork to grades two and three,
so much that they had a lot of work for the first few minutes of the day,
while Miss Nett worked with the first graders. Or, knowing Miss Nett,
she would give them something interesting to do, like looking at the globe
to find faraway places, with the best student in control (every child aspired
to being picked by Miss Nett for anything), or reading a story book from
the collection the state provided. The best was one that Nett brought from
home, from Grandpop's extensive library. These were easy-to-read books
about animals, some cloth covered and well worn, but with lots of pictures.

When Nett came back to check on the readers, she would ask questions
or give them extra information to enhance their knowledge. Anyway, they
remained quiet while the first-graders moved to the front of the room, six
at a time for recitation, spelling, or learning their reading skills. Usually,
when she moved to grade two, the first-graders practiced penmanship or
were instructed to draw a particular subject until she went back to them
after the third grade had its lessons.

Blake loved his mom and was not at all ashamed of having her as a
teacher. All the kids loved her. She was kind, sympathetic, loving, and—
well—motherly. It was nice to be her son. He was the envy of the other
kids, and he wondered if their mothers were patient like his. He was especially proud when, at the end of the day, it was story time and Mom would
read from an interesting book, one of her own. She read several chapters
a day, and the anticipation of completing a book was exciting. Her books
were *Treasure Island*, *Grimms' Fairy Tales*, *Robinson Crusoe*, and Blake's
favorite, *The Last of the Mohicans*. Indian stories were the best!

Of course, the best parts of the day were the cafeteria and recess. The
children marched in a line from their rooms down the dark hall to the
porch at the back near the bathrooms, and across to the high school side.
Then they found their places in the special section of the cafeteria reserved

for their grade, where the younger children's lunches were already in place. The older ones got in line for a plate fill-up. Everybody had the same lunch, whatever the cafeteria ladies decided to make. More often than not, it was navy beans and biscuits. On lucky days, they had fried chicken or chicken and gravy with biscuits, and bad days were pone bread made with molasses. Bad or good days always came with a glass of milk. Some wised up and brought their lunch with them in a sack. The less advantaged ones were stuck with the free lunch from the cafeteria ladies.

Food was scarce, or at least a variety of food was scarce. The mail truck could only bring in a certain amount. It was always loaded down with supplies, flour, canned and jarred goods, chicken feed in rather pretty feed bags (from whose cloth the ladies made dresses for their little girls, with Miss Odessa always getting first choice), lumber, nails, and the mail of course, plus whatever the islanders had ordered from various points on the mainland. More often than not, a visitor was also arriving, for either a fresh start at life or a job already promised. Mostly the truck carried salesmen. The rest of the food was supplied by the villages' families, who provided as much as they could spare. Nobody starved, and everybody left with a full tummy. Sometimes a dessert or a potted meat sandwich might appear if it was a really good day.

Recess after lunch was the absolute highlight of the day. All ages were used to playing with each other. It was time to get together with friends in other rooms. The high school took to the ball field, both boys and girls. There were excellent players among the girls. The elementary students played in front of the building. It was fun to look forward to being picked for a team, with notes being passed back and forth ahead of time as to who would be picked for what game. Blake always wanted to be on Luke's team, even though it was older boys. Ellie had her own set of friends. A quiet girl who dressed better than anyone else was her favorite. Her name was Nancy, and she was an only child. She and Ellie would share secrets. There was also another girl, Agnes, who was very poor, and some of the other girls did not like to play with her. But Ellie and Nancy did, so the three of them would watch and snicker together and not mind being left out of the rougher games, like Red Rover. Ellie's condition prevented her from putting herself in the position of getting hurt, so some games were out. Nancy was too clean, and Agnes was not chosen. None of them resented their position. They had each other.

Blake, of course, gravitated toward the tough games. He really got his licks when he played Red Rover, as most of the time he was chosen as the weakest link for someone to run through. But with his hand in Luke's, that proved to be a mistake. Luke would move over and take the blow, and the opposing runner had to go back where he came from. Luke's buddy Colby usually took the other side of Blake. It was a game within a game. Luke and Colby, Blake and Thomas, the playground musketeers. They did not see each other much out of school, but it was fun to know somebody who lived in the village. Colby also visited Luke at the compound. There was always a softball game, and Colby's dad played first base, so Colby got to come over.

Ellie did not have friends who visited, so she made up the fourth or sometimes the fifth guy, if Thomas was there, and kept up with whatever adventures the boys went on. She learned to catch pretty good, but her batting was a little weak. Playing on the big softball field made stars out of all of them. Luke and Blake had strong throwing arms, and Ellie could both throw and catch. Colby was good at batting and a really good fielder. There were times when the gang of them took on the Coast Guard, much to the delight of the seamen. They missed their families at home, and these kids were great fun. Once the guardsmen let the kids win, and it was a tale to tell forever. The kids didn't realize they were being used to field the balls the men from the station hit. They thought they were "in the game," and the adults encouraged every one of them that chased a foul ball or a possible home run. There were lots of hugs of appreciation at the end—even chocolate. Those guys knew how to charm a kid.

Little Blake was known as a toughie. He would excel from sheer desire, and he was always the fastest runner in a foot race. He proved to be an excellent choice when being picked for a game at school. The most anticipated game was softball, played on the back field behind the school building. When Luke got to the seventh grade, he was one of the first chosen on any team. Surprisingly, Blake was chosen also, because he could run like the wind, and some of the heavier boys would want him to run the bases. Stealing bases was his specialty. By the time recess was over, everyone was so dirty and tired that there was no trouble in the classroom, probably very little learning, and maybe lots of afternoon doze-offs.

Grandmom always anticipated what went on at school lunches and provided homemade treats for when the kids got home. Afternoon snack was important to her, and she spent as much time preparing it for the children as she did for the lunches she made for Grandpop and Bill. She must have spent her whole day going from meal to meal, thinking, working, and anticipating the happy faces that enjoyed the surprise. She also managed to clean the house and care for the chickens, but Grandpop made sure Grandmom had a local woman come in each morning to help her with her chores. Used to be that when Grandpop had the store and they lived in the village—when all their own children were being born and before he took his turn at being lightkeeper—there was a local woman who lived in the back room of the old house and helped out while Grandmom cared for eight children. But when Grandpop got the keeper's job, they locked up the old house, as most of the children were grown and had their own lives. Tommy took over the store, some went to the service, Iva married and moved away, and the rest went out to the beach to live a life around the mighty lighthouse.

The Buxton children did not ride the Commando trucks, or buses as they were called. They walked home from school. Most children had others living in their direction, and they all walked home together, one or two dropping off as they reached their houses. But the lighthouse kids walked alone, in a different direction from the village, and created as much rumpus as they could think up while on that journey. They became quite an adventurous threesome, and Luke was the leader. They talked about their days, with Blake's day always seeming to be the best because he was so carefree and everything was funny. Luke was an observer, a little quiet while at school, but the king of any softball game, thus making him a popular guy, even though he was unaware of it. He was smart and athletic and not to be messed with, as others found out when they dared to pick on Ellie.

Blake was also one not to be trucked with. He would challenge boys twice his size and would embarrass any girl who dared to hurt Ellie's feelings.

Ellie had the worst days. She was always singled out by the girls who envied her position as the little princess in Luke and Blake's world. Not having parents was the biggest point of jabbing, but Ellie was so happy with her world that she actually felt sorry for those who did not share it. Ellie had her knights in shining armor, and their names were Luke and Blake. It didn't hurt that all the Coast Guard boys were so homesick that they had made her their "little sister." Ellie was a lucky girl.

Some children have what others consider a weakness—whether physical or mental or emotional—but are blessed when they look at what they do have. They often create a much happier make-believe world for themselves, one that the jabs and insults of bullies cannot penetrate. Special children live in their own imaginative mind and do not look down on others. Disadvantaged children create inside themselves what they do not have on the outside. Their parents encourage their worth. Bullies wallow around in false importance, and their only way to rise is to stand on someone else. They do not have the originality to create on their own, so they crush creativity in others. But good thoughts always make a world better, and people who have those thoughts rise to the top.

Ellie's mind was filled with blue and silver colors. Ellie had a sixth sense about things. She truly was different. Ellie could go into her shining moments at will, feeling things that seemed strange if she tried to explain them, so she kept her thoughts to herself. Ellie heard whispers, and as she grew older she began to pay attention to them. She thought her whispers came from her own special spirit world, and she was right. When Ellie saw the wolves, especially when she was alone in the yard, they seemed to speak to her with their eyes. She did not approach them—Grandpop said not to—but she sat and stared at them from a distance. She sometimes played a game with them. Who would turn away first? She always lost. They stood quietly by—not moving, their ears erect, golden eyes fixed on hers—for such a long time that finally she would laugh out loud and say, "You win," and turn away exhausted. When she turned back, they were gone. Always the same three.

At night Ellie dreamed of the wolves. She would go through a dream portal in the form of a whirling mass of silver and blue resembling a tornado whose funnel led to a tunnel leading out to something familiar—like arching trees covered with pine needles and moss that led to a sparkling stream running underground to a grotto. She liked to take her cousins on these dream trips, because it was so much better to share good times. Her dreams were realistic and filled with strange sights like caves and waterfalls. There was usually a host to greet them—sometimes the white wolf, an Indian, a pirate, or another animal. These dreams allowed the children to live a fantasy. Ellie even liked to bring her spirit, Travis, who floated overhead in watchful concern.

Ellie was especially fascinated in her dreams by her playful romps with the deer. They were so delicate and gentle. Their eyes were kind and soft, and their little white tufted tails were always twitching. She would lie on their matted-down beds, usually in the middle of a large clump of tall grass, unseen by someone just looking straight ahead. She was introduced to their fawn, light brown with white spots, and she felt like them, with the mother deer nuzzling all three of them. Always, there was a slight silver and blue cloud around it all. And when it was almost dawn, a wolf appeared out of the shadows with a look she knew to follow, telling her to get back home before the sun came up.

When she awakened, she was not tired, but rested and happy. Christo, the rooster, was just warming up. After her dream it was pleasant to have Grandmom in her room, giving her a kiss on the forehead and letting her know that it was time to get washed up, dressed, and ready for a big breakfast before school.

No, Ellie could not be hurt by bullying. They were not as lucky as she, so she thought that maybe she could do something nice for them, to help them get over their unhappy lives. It was such a shame that everybody could not have the life and thoughts that she had. Ellie was so content.

★ 9 ★

Buckskin and Feathers

It was the hunter's moon. The sea breeze was so hard that it blew Ellie's hair sideways, stinging her face. "Holy cow! Are we having a hurricane?" cried Ellie to the others. "Go there!" She motioned toward a stand of wild scrub oak, thickly entwined, with their serpentlike limbs so tightly wound together that it was hard to distinguish one from the other. It was a favorite spot for animals seeking shelter from a sudden blow. The tops could be seen from beyond the sand hill, and the children left the beach and headed for a path through and over the dunes to the refuge on the other side.

"Let's go, Luke! C'mon, Blake!" yelled Ellie, already ahead, as she ran down the side of a bank toward the tree shelter in front. "It's calm down there!"

The two boys quickly climbed the dunes trying to catch Ellie and get to the stand of trees before the sky opened up even more. The clouds were ugly, angry, and full. She slowed down, waiting for her companions. As the boys reached the top they could see the umbrella of trees on this side of the thick Buxton Woods. Quickly they rushed down the slope to where Ellie waited. They disappeared beyond the trees and brush that were the outskirts of Buxton Woods. It was also the area that backed up to Jennette's Sedge, the outlying part of the woods, where the children were forbidden to go. . As they passed under the first set of green arms, a huge rumble of thunder, which seemed to have more than one heart, exploded with pounding cracks, followed by a piercing flash of lightning. It seemed to hit something behind them, right where they were standing only an instant before. A tree on the outer fringe of the tree line smoldered with a red glow beginning near the crack in the middle. Fire! Within minutes, even before they could tear their eyes away from the fiery tree, sheets of rain began to fall in an angry attempt to extinguish the flame. The rain beat back the effects of the lightning strike. Rain one, lightning zero. Round one.

Luke looked around, counting heads to see if they were hit. Ellie had her hand over her heart, and Blake's eyes flashed with amazement. Close! Where were they now? They burrowed farther and farther into the woods. The trees at the edge were closely entangled, and there was no clearing in which to rest. The rain was relentless, but the trees were so tightly entwined that few drops hit them. They were already soaked and did not notice the golden eyes in the forest tracking their every move.

As they reached the inner edge of the woods and taller trees, the extreme roar of the saints was heard overhead. The children had not been able to see the sky or the blue and silver cast that had suddenly appeared. Their saints were sitting on the cloud. Travis, Micah, and Brendan were plotting their first real adventure for the kids, and this storm was their introduction to dream travel.

The children mistook the roar as low, rumbling thunder and burrowed even more into the thicket to get away from it. The thundering noise was only Travis, Ellie's saint, communicating with Brendan, Blake's patron, and Micah, the one who watched over Luke. The three deities had gotten together to begin schooling the children in the powers they possessed. With a swirl of silver-beaded threads of light, sparkling sheets of transparent blue mingled with a blanket of memory dust, the wet cloud swirled in a tunnel around them. The three saints leaned on a cloud of gossamer silk, floating above the forest. They observed the children. Yes, they decided, it was time to reveal some of the special powers that would mark Ellie's life. She was old enough.

Because of the unique bond between the three young ones, the saints also were ready to give a greater insight to the two boys. They were also of the Jennette family, and while they would not have powers of their own, when they combined their thoughts with Ellie's, all three would be stronger at a task.

As Luke, Blake, and Ellie awakened to the slightly familiar undertones of a discussion, looking around they found themselves sharing a small fire with a party of Croatoan Indians seeking shelter from the same storm. The three were deep in the woods, long, tall pine trees reaching a cloud and filling the forest floor with thick pine needles. Just underneath the pine were the trunks of a huge spreading live oak, with long, thick limbs twisted in various crooks from the winds that swept the island over the years. In denser areas the smaller, thicker gray scrub oak filled in to keep the area sheltered.

The forest underbrush had been crushed by the collection of tribesmen who had stomped out a clearing between the trees. In the middle of the glade was a hole dug for a fire, with dry logs in a pyramid of warmth. A gold and silver lightning bolt traveled slowly down from the clouds above, circled the fire, and was then consumed by it. The fire gave off a series of sparks, shooting upward to the astonishment of the Indians, and they stopped their conversation to glance up at the origin of the bolt, then at the awakening children. The cedar trees were so thick, they cut the world off behind them. The rain was still coming, but the blanket of foliage was too dense to even wet the fire. Buxton Woods was the home of the Croatoan, one of three tribes of Indians who had villages on the island. These were Grandmom's people—at least half of them were.

The Indians found the children huddled against a fallen log from one of the mighty oaks. They were frightened, wet and shivering from the drenching rain. The braves had mistaken the children for refugees from the unfriendly Indian uprising taking place on Roanoke Island. Their white skin and light eyes were familiar to the natives as they had previously traded with several groups of white strangers who had landed on the island for supplies, usually en route to somewhere else. The most recent group eventually settled beyond Hatteras Island, to an island nearer the mainland, and word came to the Croatoans that the strangers had fallen prey to the wrath of unfriendly Indians over a stolen goblet. The Hatteras Island Indian leader and his band had been discussing a plan to rescue the remaining settlers. The children only stared at the husky band, reluctant to move or talk. Silently Luke reached for Ellie's hand, then Blake's, and gave a reassuring squeeze.

"We're okay. Come close," he said.

He needed to show them that he was not afraid. For the first time, Ellie and Blake realized that they knew what Luke was thinking, and they responded by relaxing in the knowledge that he was indeed in charge. If this group wanted to harm them, they were late in getting at it. The men covered the children with their own cloaks, made of hides of muskrat sewn together with a type of string. The braves were clothed from the waist down in softened deerskin. A fringe of slit deer hide had been frayed and sewn down each leg and hung loosely, flapping against their thighs as the men moved around. The horseflies and other flying insects stayed away. Because they shed their outer capes, the braves were then only protected from the weather by wide deerskin straps crisscrossed over their chests. Each had the tattoo of a paw on his right shoulder. The fire warmed them as they continued to speak in hushed tones, allowing the children to rest.

It turned out that the braves were collecting roots, muds, flowers, and berries for paint. Each man tested the dye on his arm to determine if it was the effect he wanted. The maidens in the company began to huddle over the children. They had been left too long, and the effect of being wet to start with was beginning to set in. As the others tested color after color, Luke imagined that they were either getting ready for a festival or a fight.

The three saints leaned on a cloud of translucent gossamer silk, floating above the forest. They observed what was happening below. Yes, they decided, it was time: the children were old enough. Ellie needed to come into some of her abilities. The boys needed to recognize theirs, and they all needed to find out how their combined energy reacted to a time filament.

These children all had the lineage of the first recorded settlers in the New World, and also that of the first natives inhabiting the island. The combination was unusually rare, as this bloodline could be unhealthy, but in these three, it was abnormally thick and rich. In this line from Grandmom, the women passed the blood tendencies on to their off-spring. Historically the male was only the carrier of the line, never the recipient of its qualities. Only the female would demonstrate gifts of the blood, not the males. But not with this family. Annie had taken the brunt of the combination of weakness and strength the legacy had to offer. She did not survive. But the children, through their mothers, had been dealt a different set of the combined two and had inherited unusual power—a power that only showed itself every hundred years or so.

In the forest, where every sound was frightening, and everything that moved a potential predator, the three sensed protection. Glancing around, they found it. Peering from the shadows of the thick brush were several sets of fluorescent golden eyes, narrowed in anticipation of being needed. Grandpop had always said the wolves would be there to protect them. Had the wolves followed the children through the dream portal?

The conversation among the men was animated, sometimes angry and getting louder, but it was not directed toward the children. It concerned an unseen enemy. The men paid little attention to the wet, shivering huddle, until one of the Indian maidens noticed that they were visibly trembling, even under the mound of fur. They were uncontrollably cold and still drenching wet. She called out to the leader.

In a swoop the youngsters were startled to find themselves safely cradled in the sides of a burly man covered all over in deer hide. He had a different look. The cloth of his cape was so soft and dry, the raindrops only beaded up and then dropped to the ground without soaking into the hide. Luke snuggled in. He was soaked to the bone with his hands at his sides, completely covered by the big Indian. Ellie was the same, shaking uncontrollably against the huge figure. Blake could hardly hold his bones together, as he clutched to the chest of the husky dark man. Being in his huge arms was like sitting on a tree limb. Body heat was comforting in more ways than one. It was also an assurance of acceptance.

This meeting was their first introduction to Manteo, the son of the matriarch of the Croatoans, Weroansqua. Again the young Indian maiden stepped forward and reached out her hand to Ellie. In her hand was a warm deerskin hide, lined fully on the inside with gray rabbit fur. Ellie folded herself in the cozy blanket and surveyed her surroundings. Huddled under the cloak, which she had pulled over her head, she was free to observe her hosts.

Manteo had long, dark, shining hair. It was thick and heavily braided down one side, with long turkey and pheasant feathers woven throughout. At the end of his braid was the down of a snow goose. His head was encircled by a band of deerskin, and dangling at the edges of the ties were small white cowrie shells. He had a dark tattoo of the wolf's paw behind his right shoulder, indicating his tribe. He was taller than most of the others. His cape was several deerskins stitched together, casually slung over his shoulder and falling to his knees. He was bare-chested except for a wide crisscross deer hide strapping across his brown chest. He was wearing deerskin trousers, and laced all the way from his knees to the tops of his hide boots were more straps. Nothing could penetrate his leggings.

The beautiful young maiden who so generously wrapped Ellie against her bone-chilling shivering was Manteo's younger sister, Sooleawa (meaning silver in their language). She, too, was adorned with cascades of bright feathers, shells in her hair, and pearls hanging from her neck and ears. Wrapped from her wrists almost to the elbow was a thin cloth of hide, with shell and pearl bracelets stitched casually around the cuff. The maiden was the most magical vision Ellie had ever seen. Her dark hair was straight and almost reached her waist. Oiled, it carried a soft scent. Her dress was simple deer hide beaten and worked to a soft, loosely drifting cloth, and she easily moved in it to accomplish her chores. Her leggings were also bound with straps reaching the tops of her boots. Ellie thought it must be easy to walk in that covering of hide, guarded against worrying about stepping on something foreign. The forest hid many dangers above and below. The young maiden took the wary girl by the hand and gently nudged her forward.

One of the braves picked up Blake, hoisting him to his shoulders. Blake's heart skipped several beats as he rode atop this wide-shouldered young man. Blake kept his eyes forward, as the gangly young brave strode through the forest without a thought of his charge being hit by a low-hanging limb. That was Blake's responsibility, and it eventually became a game of duck and don't fall off. Manteo put his arm around Luke and shared his wide cape with the boy. They walked as one. They all headed for the high piney ridge, to the underground caves and Manteo's lodge.

The Indian brave on whose shoulders Blake perched was Manteo's younger brother, Wematin. All the children were being claimed by members of the same family, which meant that they would not be apart from each other. They would all be bedded in the same longhouse.

The Croatoan lived in scattered lodges framed with bent sapling poles covered with bark, hide, and tightly woven reeds and grasses. Each had a smoke hole in the middle to accommodate the fire that was used for cooking and, in the winter, warmth. In the summer, the walls could be lifted for the breezes to float through. Around the edges of the walls were baskets full with supplies, bowls, twines, and unfinished hides. Also lining the walls and around the fire were platforms covered with soft furs and mats for sleeping. Most houses sheltered one extended family. Some were smaller and only housed a few people. Each unit had its own fire and could be private if need be. There could be as many as five families living in one long, partially enclosed lodge. Everywhere in the village and near the lodges, a citronella plant smoldered, giving off smoke that kept away flying and biting insects.

Manteo's dwelling was extremely long. It had three fires. Platform beds lined the walls and sitting areas around the fire. Manteo; his mother, Weroansqua; sister, Sooleawa; brother, Wematin; his mother's brother, Loutau (meaning fire); and now three English children would occupy this lodge. There were longer lodges, built half in and half out of the hills. They were communal, mostly for single warriors and tradesmen. The shaman lived inside the cave. His residence had two separate entrances, one in front and one that came out the back of the cave. If he needed to wander in the woods, it was a solitary move. He was never bothered. One had to request an audience to approach the shaman.

They walked through the village into a huge clearing. At the side of the clearing was another specific area with several thick, straight poles in a circle. On each pole was carved a mask of varying expressions—angry, angelic, mirthful, celebratory, and warlike. In the middle of the compound a communal fire blazed. The houses were designed to rotate out from this fire. All ceremonies were held in this central place. There were racks along the outskirts of the clearing that were used for several things: drying fish and drying and mending nets.

Also located off the main area were covered arched structures whose sides were open. Beside each covering on the ground were huge wooden logs, carved out in the middle to create a vessel designed to catch rain. The women did their work here—making food, preparing food for storage, mending hides, or making the many-sized baskets used in daily living. The women did their work together, as most everything in the tribe was done in the company of others. Living conditions were comfortable.

Built among the trees were walkways and platforms. The platforms had patchy roofs and walls, as nothing was completely enclosed. These were places of refuge from the tides, animals, and unwelcome company. Surrounding the sound side of the encampment was a tall palisade made of stripped trees and held together with vine. The palisade was so far inland from the sound that the structure could not be seen from the water. The Indians had learned—from their sightings of ships and sporadic visits from strange people—that it was now necessary to protect themselves from possible enemies.

Warring tribes didn't usually bother with the Croatoan. What did anyone gain by attacking a small village on an island? They hardly had enough food to sustain themselves. Thinking they had anything worth stealing, except for their women, was folly. Croatoan women were unusually striking. But the Croatoan commonly solved this problem with trade and wampum. The hill, woods, and huge sand dunes protected the back of the village, shielding it from intruders. The natives did not expect an assault from the sea.

Meeting Weroansqua—Manteo's mother, the head of the Croatoan—was the most astonishing event of all. She was regal. She was handsome—not pretty, but striking—and splendid. She carried herself like a deer, with slow and deliberate movements. Every motion was planned. She was tall—which accounted for her children's height—and truly the most majestic of the tribe. Her hair was still dark, with streaks of gray around the temples. It was full and curly, and when untied it fell down her back. She wore a wide band of hide across her forehead. The band was rigid, so it stood up on her head like a crown. In the middle of the band was an iridescent pin shell, with a large, irregular pearl in the center. She wore a loose-fitting deer hide tunic that touched the floor. Her boots were like those of her tribe, with straps binding up to her knees. Their breeding showed. As with the wolves, it came through in their attitude.

Weroansqua was especially interested in Ellie and seemed to know her and be familiar with her already. Ellie was also interested in Weroansqua, and wondered if the Indian could see into the future, as Ellie knew she, herself, was now existing in the past. It was like Weroansqua was talking to her own noble daughter when she spoke to Ellie. Strangely, Ellie had an understanding of the Indian dialect spoken around her. Weroansqua trusted Ellie only to her daughter, Sooleawa. The leader needed to impart wisdom to both of them. Ellie was the future.

The Croatoan believed in the immortality of the soul. The tribe believed that, upon death, the soul either entered the heavens to live with the gods or was placed near the setting sun called Popogusso to burn eternally in a huge pit. Weroansqua was given the position of matriarch when her husband was wounded by a wild boar on a hunting trip across the sound. The boar ripped into the old chief's belly, exposing his entrails, and the wound could not be closed. He was carried back across the sound to the village. At the funeral, the shaman saw in the fire that Weroansqua should be appointed leader. He knew of her special powers and her connection to the lost continent, and he welcomed the added knowledge. He saw her not as competition but as an ally.

The Croatoan chose their priests for knowledge and wisdom and held them as leaders of their religion. They went to the shaman for advice and for punishment. There were also the conjurers, who were chosen for their magical abilities. They were thought to have powers from a personal connection with a supernatural being—mostly spirits from the animal world. Healing was handled by the shaman. Conjurors were used when the tribe anticipated war. The shaman was occupied at all times in the understanding of natural things—air, water, plants, wind, sea creatures, animals, birds, and fire were all studied to discover how they could enhance the tribe.

Sooleawa recognized in Ellie a kindred spirit. She and Ellie sought the guidance of Weroansqua, this woman who was connected to the white wolf. Ellie had seen the wolf as she entered the longhouse, and she smiled at Luke and Blake, who also recognized this as a sign that they were among family. The wolf was lazily stretched out near the platform by the fire, giving only an unconcerned glance at the strangers. His eyes never left Ellie, and she could hardly tear her eyes away from him. Weroansqua had planned this meeting with the shaman for a long time. They expected the children, ever since Manteo knew he needed to help his new English friends across the sound. Finding the children answered the mystery in the shaman's fire several nights ago. They were to receive help from "those who came from the rain." History would not be bent, but it could be smoothed.

The children slept soundly, and they awakened to discover the beautiful buckskin clothing soft, dry, and comfortable. The flapping fringe everywhere served to discourage the mosquitoes and flies that roamed the forest and swamps of the hidden village. The children settled into the Croatoan camp with ease.

Wematin, Manteo's brother, was so captivated with Blake that he took him everywhere he went. Both boys were impressed with Wematin. He was more fun than the other braves, younger than Manteo, and such a large, strapping young man. He had mastered knife throwing, hatchet throwing, and the bow and arrow, and with whips of rawhide he could remove anything with a flick. He could easily wrestle to the ground all other boys his age, and some older, with no loss of teeth or limb. His skill with a bow could not be matched, not even by Manteo. He was Manteo's pride and joy. But he was a young pup who didn't think he needed his brother for fun, so Manteo saw in Luke another successful protégé and looked forward to teaching him, as he had done Wematin.

Wematin set about instructing Blake while Manteo taught Luke. This friendly competition was thrilling to the boys. They were learning many things that they had never even seen. Blake mastered the art of throwing the knife, but the hatchet was too heavy. Luke was especially interested in the whip. He eventually could snatch the knife out of Blake's hand. All the while, the night was spent around the fire listening to the plans of the braves as they mapped out the rescue of the strangers across the huge space of water called a sound.

A sound is a body of water not entirely open to the sea, and sometimes it connects two bodies of water. It is named a "sound" because of the uneven bottom—shallow in some parts, deep in others—making it necessary to drop something in the water to determine by "sound" the water's depth.

Ellie spent her time with Weroansqua and Sooleawa, learning of the mysteries of her ancestors. Weroansqua was especially anxious to sit with Sooleawa, as her beautiful daughter was to be married as soon as all the commotion of the "rescue" had died down. It seemed that Sooleawa was only interested in glances from her betrothed, and the giggling of the other girls increased as marriage talk became paramount. Time was slipping away from Weroansqua as Sooleawa had not been instructed about the legacy. Sooleawa seemed so willing to listen, though, when Ellie was around. Weroansqua had longed for time alone with her daughter, and now with this new child, the time was awarded.

"You both need to understand that you are special," Weroansqua began. "We are women who have special blood. Yes, Ellie, you are of this family. You are not the child of the settlers on the island across the sound, as we have allowed others to believe. It is fine for them to think that, but I must instruct you differently. I am gifted with the ability to understand what is in another's mind. If I concentrate, I know what a person is thinking, even if that person does not utter a word. Sooleawa, you also can penetrate another's mind, but Ellie, your powers are stronger. I can feel it."

Ellie had trouble understanding how she could fit into this life she had only been introduced to a few days before.

"Ellie, you are connected to both of us by blood. Your grandmother, Odessa, is also one of my daughters. She, and you as her granddaughter, were descended from Sooleqwa's daughter Jenet (the name later evolved to Jennette), who married an Englishmen. So her child was half Indian and half English. We will have many daughters in the future, but the past is what guides us. Sooleawa, you are able to recognize others' thoughts, but Ellie, you will be able to know the thoughts of humans and animals." Ellie gasped at what the old woman was telling her, characteristically putting her hand over her mouth and listening intently. How would she tell Luke and Blake? Still, this news was almost a relief for her to hear. She had long known that she could read the minds of others, but she kept it to herself. Sometimes she thought of it as dreaming. Her dreams were vivid. She could lose something, find it in a dream, and then recover it when she awakened. She also knew inside when Luke or Blake were on their way to her. She sensed things. She knew the minds of the wolves, the deer, and the squirrels, but those were dreams, she told herself. Could it happen when she was awake also?

"Luke and Blake, do they also have the power? They are of the same blood," Ellie asked timidly.

"They do, but only around you. You are the conductor of thought between the members of the bloodline, and the boys, through their grandmother, are of your blood. But they depend on you, as yours is the strongest heart in our line—at least it will be when my own blood leaves my body."

Weroansqua wondered if the child truly understood the treasure she carried from her mother. Annie's blood had transferred this gift to Ellie, and it was a concentration of great strength—but just for Ellie, not Annie.

Yes, the adventure began at the first raindrop. The children were transported by their mischievous spirits to experience the beginning of their own family. This island family that had existed for close to 400 years—whose ancestry was 10,000 years old—was keeping a secret, a secret that now had to come to light. Weroansqua would talk more to Sooleawa and Ellie, but little by little. It was a lot to take in. Time revealed all, and it would take much time.

The clearing where the Croatoan had the concentration of their village was rich in foliage. The woods were covered in moss and vine that made everything so green. The moss grew up most of the trees, as there was a freshwater spring that shot up through the hill and around which the tribe had built a dam to hold the water spurting up from the gusher. They drew cooking and drinking water from the well, and also watered their abundant harvest of corn, squash, greens, sweet potatoes, melons, blueberries, strawberries, and blackberries.

The children were given a tour of the village. Wematin did not want them to get lost, and he was proud to show the children where to hide if something should merit it. Underground on the hill, a path was covered in dead leaves, and torches lit the way. The walls were held together by the packed sand, mixed with crushed shells, lime from across the sound, and mud from the marshes. The soft bottom was like walking on plush earth, and once in a while it was necessary to step over fallen limbs, which had allowed a pattern of light to appear through the thick leaves of the trees overhead. The roof was made of thickly woven marsh grasses, laced with palmetto leaves, and huge ferns grew on the forest floor. The roots of trees laced through the packed mud, making the overhead sturdy. There were spots of blue sky when looking up.

Then they came upon another small cave leading deeper into the hill—a wolf burrow, perfectly hidden by a fallen tree. As the journey continued, there were wide archways that originated at the beginning of a long hall leading to the network of houses on levels, with walkways and stairs into the tall trees, to make a connection of bridges and steps that led to higher ground if need be. The branches were lashed together with vines and limbs pulled tightly to create walls and structures that withstood the shifting sand that threatened to overtake the island. The sand created a tall dune, hiding the village even more. This huge wall of earth also protected against ocean overwash.

Now, after hundreds of years, the shifting of the island sands had covered over the trees and created caves of the structures underneath. The children had stumbled into Old Buxton.

But the animals knew. They even went there to ride out storms. Old Buxton was a village petrified in time, made by the constant pressure of the surrounding hill and its vegetation. The weight served to make the structural beams of this old village even stronger. A small stream ran through the corner of the village, where the gusher runoff came down through the upper level and created a waterfall in the underground grotto. The stream was passable from side to side by rope bridges. They came up for air in several places and continued on, the rush of water running deep. Some said the water was a tributary of the river running through the ocean. The water also ran through a natural filter, somewhere above ground, and the deeper it went, the fresher the water was.

The wolves ruled Old Buxton. They were generous in their territory, but they still ruled. They ruled it during Indian time, and through the years they were overseers to the spirit of the forest. This was the tribe of the wolf. Most Indian tribes identified with an animal spirit. For the Croatoans the wolf was the sign of protection, and it had an advantage over other deities because the raven was its constant companion. The raven could see what was to come, and as a companion to the wolf, the wolf was then prepared for anything. The pack was seldom seen. Even the white wolf was only seen inside the lodge of Weroansqua. Manteo, Sooleawa, and Wematin did not speak of it. Learning this, the children began to understand their own connection to the wolf.

In the woods was plenty of room for buildings and trails. Even as everything had been covered with branches, the pine needle paths among the trees gave a feeling of familiarity that was comforting.

The children knew that they had been here before. They wandered through the web of rooms and buildings, watching the life of the people who had taken them in. Some were chewing the deer hide to make it supple. Some were bringing in firewood to stack by the hearth. Others crafted mats and baskets, and some etched designs into the outer wall of a newly cast clay pot. Everyone was busy. There were no idle hands. The community of Croatoans welcomed the children, thinking that they were ones who had been saved from the Roanoke.

They met the old shaman, Powwaw. He was a wise old man. His hair was long and white, braided on both sides, and hung with heron feathers. He wore a woven cloth made from the bark and striplings of trees. It was purple and red, and certain panels showed white painted figures: the turtle, the raven, the shark, the owl, the snake, and the wolf. Each symbol was a god he acknowledged for the strength each particular one had for the earth. The turtle held the earth up on its back, the raven saw the future, the shark was the predator, the owl was wise, the snake was cunning, and the wolf was the protector of all. The wolf and the raven were particularly good friends and always were seen together, or not far apart.

Luke spent most of his time with Powwaw. He followed the shaman into the woods on his quest to find healing herbs nestled on the forest floor. He collected muds from certain streams and berries from particular trees. Some fruit he left alone as being poisonous. Specific flowers were necessary to boil with mixtures of saps and oils from bushes and trees. On some days, Luke and Powwaw poled around the edges of the island in a small dugout canoe, looking for grasses and plants that grew near the bank. Powwaw would stand at one end of the dugout and stick the pole in the mud, walk toward the other end, unslop the pole, and walk slowly to and past the pole, moving the boat along, looking down all the way. Luke was looking also, but he only saw colorful minnows and tiny crabs. It was an interesting day with Powwaw. The old Indian talked the whole time, describing the habits of every animal they saw. Luke could understand by the signs Powwaw made with his hands. Luke became so familiar with the old man that he would just think of a question and Powwaw would answer. Luke's blood was working also, and the old shaman knew it.

After those excursions, Luke helped the old Indian get his precious treasures to his area of the village. Perched on the hearth, he watched while Powwaw began to cook up his concoctions, chanting and breathing in vapors all the time. At those times, when Powwaw was so deep into himself, Luke went to other hearths and listened to stories or watched the men wrap the handles of their spears and knives. He and Blake visited one man, Mingan (meaning gray wolf) who constantly carved small wolves and staffs from beautiful wood. The wolves looked so real, but they were also so very small. They lined the walls of his hut on strings of grass. The staffs were covered all the way down with ornate carvings or a special knob fashioned with a bird's beak, bear's head, or snake's head for a handle, all leaning against every wall in Mingan's dwelling. Many liked the staffs as they sometimes needed balance while trying to pick their way through the forest. Blake was so taken with the figurines that his eyes gave him away. The old man offered him one.

"Should I take it?" he asked Luke.

"Of course. It is a sign of friendship. The wolf is considered sacred to this group, and they live peacefully with them." Luke had learned much from Powwaw.

A pack of wolves watched the tribe from the shadows of the trees. At night the children could hear them howl at the moon. It was a single, long howl, then silence, then another howl of a different pitch, then silence, until all of them had their turn. It was an eerie and comforting sound that the children went to sleep with most nights at home, so this was familiar—a little bit of a symphony to add to the constant croaking frogs, the chirping crickets, and the continuous ringing of the cicadas that filled the night. Sometimes there was a slap of the sound against a faraway bank, but no ocean roar. They were too far away—far away from where they started.

It was dusk on the night Manteo approached the three travelers and beckoned for them to follow him. They knew something was afoot. Ellie was then wrapped securely in deer hide from head to toe, and she wore the special boots that she had admired on the other Indians. Luke and Blake were also covered in thick clothing, their faces painted black. The hunter's moon was shining with just enough glow to light their way through the trees. The spirits added a silver haze, and golden eyes glimmering behind the trees surely added light to the path. The children followed the braves to the waiting dugouts in the sound. These were the larger ones, not the ones used for fishing. These dugouts could seat over thirty rowers but could carry more, and they had multiple paddles stretched across the seats. There were seven canoes. As the Indians began to climb into their respective places on the crafts, each of the children was motioned to board separate dugouts. The leader of the boat stood at the long rudder handle, and either Luke, Ellie, or Blake sat in front of him. Manteo was in one, Sooleawa another, and Wematin in another. Manteo said to each of the children, "We will meet those of your tongue, and you will tell them our heart."

They were not exactly clear as to the meaning, but the children trusted Manteo, so they sat quietly and listened. They were also filled with thoughts to, from, and of each other. They were going to translate to these strangers the Croatoan were meeting. But this was some kind of secret—maybe even a little dangerous.

Luke shot out a thought to the others: "Do not be afraid. Look how many braves are here." Luke was confident and curious. He felt very comfortable with Manteo. He was like Uncle Jack and Lindy in one person. Luke wanted to show Manteo that he understood the training, as Manteo wanted him to be a brave. Luke wanted to meet that challenge. He felt inside that he was in a book he read. He was living a book, and he couldn't dream of the adventures he would later experience. It was hard to believe this one. But meeting and having a friendship with a man like Manteo weighed heavily on Luke. He really did want to succeed in his own mind. How exciting this was, and how important to be calm. Yes, Luke was scared, but only on the inside. With the big Indian's hand on his shoulder as he turned to go to his own boat, everything relaxed, and Luke became the young man on whom Manteo would depend.

Blake said, "I'm okay," while holding his arms across his chest. He was dressed in armor, so there was no mistaking what might happen here. He was scared, but he fought it. He so wanted to be his best—not *the* best, but *his* best. He had the great, calm feeling that he was not alone. He knew Wematin would not let anything happen to him, and Wematin was strong. But there was something else. His brother was with him, and he also knew that he could do anything a girl could do—and Ellie wasn't crying. So Blake decided his attitude when he was scared was to be comfortable and curious and watch what was going on. Life was cool.

Ellie was also thinking calm thoughts. She was flushed under all that deer hide. But as Weroansqua oversaw Ellie's dressing by the young maiden, Weroansqua had told the maiden that Ellie was not to be scratched by bushes or briars. "Cover her!" Ellie was special, and everyone treated her so. The maiden complied.

Ellie saw the beautiful silky dark water and the sky vibrant in the colors of evening. She knew she was of the pack and that they would protect her. And there were so many packs around her: the Indians, her cousins, the wolves, and for some reason, the sky.

It was a beautiful sight—seven canoes in a row and eight painted, armed, heavily clad shadows in each boat. Everybody was so dark, but the sound was slick with traces of red and blue as the clouds went away, leaving lines of purple and pink on the water topped by a gold border of leftover sun settling below the horizon. The water was glossy looking, no waves. This was going to be an endless ride. They all paid attention to their surroundings. It was necessary to remember all this as they felt the presence of their spiritual guides. Even looking across the sound, directly into the setting sun slipping down below the water, the colors of the spirits were there—their bluish cast shot with silver. The billowing clouds floating across the top of the water line did not go away. They stayed until the children dozed off as the dark relaxed the colors of the day.

The Croatan were bringing visitors back to the village.

⋆ 10 ⋆

The Rescue

They rowed for four hours. Steady, hard pulls, quiet, the splash of the paddles dipping down in unison, and the paddles coming out in the same rhythm—repeat, repeat, soothing and relaxed. All the children slept with the sound of the water rippling in their dreams. The gentle slap of the water against the boat, the smooth slide of the paddles in and out of the dark pool, was mesmerizing. The moon licked the peaks of the tides and danced around the spray. Although the three slept soundly, once in a while they awakened and as they strained to see what was cloaked in darkness, a turtle drifted by, and a school of fish looked fluorescent against the moon's light. The braves were steady and seemed not to tire. Each was moving to the soft beat of the coxswain leading the count. They did not dare make a sound. This was a mission of danger, as the children had guessed while walking down to the sound.

Manteo had explained to the three visitors while sitting cross-legged around a circle in the main lodge what had been seen in the fire days ago, before the rain. The Croatoan were looking for a sign to help them with their mission. The spirit spoke to Powwaw and said that help would come from the children of the rain.

When Manteo and his braves reached their destination, they pondered the dilemma. There were strangers who came from across the ocean in the horizon the Indians called Dawnland. Manteo knew them, spent time with them, learned their language, visited their queen, traveled across the big water and lived with them in their compound, and helped them adapt to the strange world they had chosen to adopt. A misunderstanding had taken place between the settlers and the local Indians. Upon hearing this, Manteo was fearful that the new visitors were about to come in harm's way. This danger had become imminent, and the Indians consulted their Great Spirit to reveal a plan to bring the settlers to safety. They thought the children were the answer, as they were considered a calming force to convince the ragged survivors that these Indians were taking them out of potential danger and into friendly hands. The settlers already knew Manteo, but this many Indians could be overwhelming to the bedraggled colonists. At this point, the settlers did not know whom to trust. They had trusted Wanchese, and he had betrayed them. Why would they think that Manteo was any different?

When Manteo and his braves reached their destination, they pulled their canoes into hiding under a huge overhang of scrub oak, water oaks, willow trees, and tall marsh grass. Everyone motioned for quiet, and the Indian braves grabbed their clubs, hatchets, knives, and bows and crawled out of the canoes, dropping down into the marsh. Several braves stood back waist deep in the reeds, watching as the others disappeared into the thick brush. The coxswain and each child were motioned to stay. Manteo wanted to survey the situation for enemy scouts, not wanting the children involved if there was immediate danger. Blake tried to signal Luke, but his handler gently covered his mouth to stifle the sound. Only the frogs, a few marsh chucks, and crickets were making noise. Luke spied a large owl high atop one of the trees, but the owl just stared and did not make his usual sound. The watcher of the night—what had he seen?

The brush parted, and the children were motioned forward. Several Indians appeared from the reeds to accompany the three youngsters to the waiting rescue party. The group advanced as the way was cleared. There was just enough moon to distinguish a moving object. The braves made no sound of breath or foot. Crouched and guided by a steady hand, Luke, Ellie, and Blake carefully half crawled through the thick forest. Ellie was glad to have her legs and feet laced against the sharp edges of the marsh grass. In anticipation of the struggle through the brush, Weroansqua had instructed for Ellie's locks to be braided so that her hair would not get caught in the bushes. Her whole head was wrapped, and Weroansqua had smeared a portion of the wrap with tree fungus to keep away the black flies and mosquitoes.

Across the chests of everyone, including the children, was a vest of heavily woven reed tied on both sides. The vest was actually two pieces—one covered the chest, the other covered the back. This was a caution against arrows that were surely going to fly. The chest plates of Manteo and the braves were painted. Some had figures, some painted designs, some had chosen animals of bravery. The heavy hide crisscrossing their chests protected the skin against the rough armor of reeds. Their faces were painted black outlined in dark red, with white around their eyes to look as menacing as possible. They were oiled against both insects and battle, with war paint covering their arms. The faces of the children were also painted black. The entire company intended to get lost in the darkness. This was an adventure to top all adventures.

Ellie decided that this was the perfect time to try out the information that Weroansqua had given her. Everything was so intense, the air was alive with silence. As the Indians moved noiselessly through the thick brush and grass, Ellie concentrated on a thought to Luke.

"Are you afraid?" she felt herself sending.

Luke quickly turned around as if he had been struck by an arrow. He looked at her strangely and shook his head, "No."

Ellie smiled behind her black face, and then with a smirk she thought, *I'll try Blake.*

"Are you afraid?" she concentrated hard, not closing her eyes because the reeds and bushes were so thick that she was afraid she would stumble.

"Are you afraid?" she repeated in her mind, focusing on Blake.

Blake took it to the next level by thinking, "Are you?"

"No," she responded, hoping he wouldn't pick up her anxious reply.

"Me neither," he shot back. He began to step more lively and actually turned his crouch into a more erect bearing. Blake's little heart seemed to be the strongest of all.

The golden eyes that watched did not appear to be kind. Their own wolves had not crossed the sound, so the children kept quiet and close. They followed as best they could the primitive path that the Croatoan provided, noticing that their handlers looked around suspiciously for anyone in pursuit.

Finally they saw the jagged solid wall of sticks looming against the night, and they knew it was the fort of either friend or foe. They were hardly breathing as Manteo pushed open the gate to the stockade and stepped in. He looked around and motioned for the others to get quickly inside the wall as he began to look for the settlers.

When all were safely behind the wall, the children also glanced around, but not for settlers. They were just curious to see what was there.

Luke whispered to Ellie, "I think I heard a message from you, but not in my ear, in my mind. Did you send me a message from your mind? Because Powwaw and I have tried it, and we can, and I felt the same strong feeling I did with Powwaw."

Ellie reached out for Blake to come near, but before she could speak with him, Manteo discovered the settlers' hiding place. There was much commotion and excitement in seeing him. Manteo motioned for the Croatoan to kneel in a show of comradeship to the startled colonists. He had been right. This many Indians—in full war paint, carrying weapons— was almost more than the settlers could take.

While the company was recovering from their shock, Ellie and Blake had a chance to observe their surroundings. They were behind a circular wall of what had been tall trees, stripped of their limbs and bark, that made up the sides of the fort. Their houses were more sophisticated than those of the Croatoan. They looked more permanent. The walls were made of wooden logs, and the roof of each house was pitched rather than rounded. The structures also had square window openings, no glass, that could be shut off by pulling down a heavy hide. There was one large house in the middle, and others surrounded it. There was no ceremonial clearing in the center. A type of open shed displayed a work area where logs were shaped and furniture was made. They, too, had large racks for mending and drying nets. There were wooden barrels with iron wraps holding the planks in place. Inside the shed was a huge bellows for melting iron and other metals. Tables had been made from sawed-off tree trunks. It was truly different from the Indian village they had just left.

Ellie felt sorry for the Indians. They had so little but were so generous, and here they were trying to help a people who had come into their world carrying the trappings of a much richer society. She wondered why they did not share with the Croatoan. This whole situation was backward. Her heart was with whom she now knew were her people, but she thought, *Both are my people. I am English also.*

The settlers hesitated, still afraid that Manteo had come to finish what Wanchese had started. Manteo signaled for Luke to step forward. Luke stood erect beside Manteo and waited for an indication from his mentor. Manteo knelt down beside Luke and told him in broken English what to say. The English were once again taken aback by the small thin boy in blackface, standing straight while the huge Indian spoke softly to him.

"We have come to rescue you," Luke said confidently, and continued, "It is urgent. We must go now!" Then he stopped and looked at Manteo.

What was this little English boy doing here, they thought, *and look how friendly he appeared with the mighty brave—and he was speaking English.* Also, there were two more children. One might be a girl.

The men gathered their thoughts quickly. The message was clear, and the reassurance that it was delivered by an English boy and an Indian was beginning to sink in, as was the urgency. Silent hands reached out for Manteo, and the eager Englishmen surrounded the tall Indian and his young lad.

There were fourteen women, forty-one men, nine children, and one baby left in the palisade. Some had gone west and others with Ralph Lane, one of the settlers. Manteo turned to Luke and stepped away with him. The colonials followed as Ellie and Blake motioned with their fingers against their lips that silence was most important. Everyone was aware that Wanchese and his braves could be watching, and they might not be willing to let the settlers go.

There had been a conflict between the Indians on Roanoke Island and the English who were struggling in the cocoon of a colony. An Indian had been accused of stealing a silver cup from Ralph Lane, the colony's self-appointed head. Lane had killed the man, a relative of the great chief Wingina—chief of the Roanoke, Wanchese's tribe. Wanchese was also married to Wingina's sister. The Indians were beginning to retaliate, and several colonial men had already been beheaded.

Lane had taken some men and gone north, leaving the original settlers without protection. Manteo intended to remove the colonists from peril by taking them to Hatteras Island.

Originally, when the ship landed bringing the new settlers—before they ever saw Roanoke Island—they first landed on Hatteras Island, and they met and were fed by the Croatoan. They were given water and supplies for their new home across the sound. This rescue was a reunion of sorts. The settlers knew Manteo. He had been baptized at the same ceremony as the new baby, Virginia. He was a friend and a needed refuge at this time. Manteo was now the leader, not the Englishman.

Ellie whispered to Blake, "I have something to tell you, but we don't have time now. Can you wait 'til we get back?"

"Did you talk to me? Back there?" Blake was never one to hold back anything, and he was squinting his eyes at Ellie in a very suspicious manner.

"Yes, but I need to explain," said Ellie. "I will tell you and Luke later, when we get back."

"I can do it, too." Blake was insistent on getting his words in, but he knew this was not the time. Also, standing here talking to Ellie, he was missing all the excitement. *Look at Luke*, he thought. *He is talking to the other guys. I want to do that.*

The colonists began to gather up things they could not leave behind. They took as many tools as they could carry. Axes were the main thing. The Indians did not have much metal, and it was always a thing to trade, but they were needed now. Most of what they took was in anticipation of starting a new life. They did not concern themselves with food or water, which left room for things they could not get unless a ship came from England. They had been waiting for that to happen, but it did not. The colonists were swift and silent. Each man knew without hesitation what to grab. As each was ready, they gathered at the gate of the stockade.

Manteo knelt down and touched the ground around the fort, motioning for the group to go more to the right of where they had entered. He did not want to leave a heavy trail of broken grass and twisted limbs. Advancing through the underbrush would be less noticeable than adding to the damage by going back over the same path again—and this time with more people, ones not trained in the art of covering their tracks. So Manteo took a completely different way back to the waiting canoes. The children kept close to Wematin and Sooleawa. Wematin had a firm grip on Blake. They were determined to keep up. Sooleawa grasped Ellie to keep her on her feet. Ellie could feel the low-hanging tree limbs tearing at her head covering. She was wrapped tightly all over her body. Weroansqua knew better than anyone the danger of Ellie receiving a cut, and to her, Ellie was the future. Weroansqua honored Ellie, but the little girl was quite unaware of how much.

The colonials were pressed to stay in step with the others. Once the woman with the baby tripped over a root, but Manteo caught her arm and righted her. Still no sounds were made, and this path seemed to be turning into more marsh than woods. Ellie was not fond of this place, with the glistening spiderwebs and insects that wanted to bite her. But she was brave and hurried along. After all, no one else was complaining. Concealing the large group began to get more difficult without trees. They were wondering if Manteo had taken them to a more dangerous place, one without a protective cover.

The scouts in front stopped cold. Manteo did the same, as did everyone else. The forest froze. In the quiet they could hear muffled voices. The sounds were far away, shouting excitedly. The enemy could not have seen them. It sounded like they were chasing something—possibly a deer or a wild boar. It was nearing dawn, when some animals feed. The company of intruders struggled to extract themselves from the danger that was bound to come if they did not reach the water before the hunters did. The dark of night was slipping away from them. Still, they could not hack away at the green twisted wall. They had to pick their way around it or leave it untouched in its natural state. It would be dangerous if Wanchese's men found either path—the one leading to or away from the fort. Either way, it would be obvious that the colony had help, which could only be Manteo. Before they left the fort, the party had planned to make it look like they had gone with Ralph Lane and his men, possibly north.

With a signal from Manteo, the Indian leaders began to branch out and move their charges in different directions, always heading toward the water and away from the encroaching sounds of men. As long as there were enough men to move the canoes, it did not matter where the colonials reached the water's edge—just that they reached it. The boats could move up the bank until each group was collected. Luke, Blake, and Ellie were then separated. As the groups got smaller, they drew closer to the Indians leading them and began to understand the risk they were all taking. The colonial children had been divided into three of the groups, the ones including the guardian children. This move proved to be smart, as the English children mimicked the movements of the ones leading them. Once a young boy began to sob softly, and Luke moved by his side. Luke put his arm around the boy to comfort him and, with his finger to his lips, reminded the boy to make no sounds. As the marsh grass became shorter, the bushes and trees disappeared near the water, and the groups were forced to crawl in order not to be seen. Dawn was coming, and they were in danger of the light exposing the company to the enemy. They could only move at a slow pace. They also did not want to roust any birds, as that indicated in the sky that a disturbance was ahead. Birds do not usually fly at night, so the cover of darkness had several advantages.

Luke shot a thought toward Blake. He was worried about his little brother, and along with his newly discovered abilities—thinking with Powwaw, and then Ellie—he was beginning to grasp the significance of this unbelievable adventure. Being able to contact his cousin and brother without speaking was a gift he would definitely practice once all this was over. Hopefully, he would live to do it.

"Blake, you okay?" he thought, concentrating as hard as he could and repeating the question over and over, hoping for a response. This was a long shot, but he had to try.

"I'm the best hider in this group, and I don't break any twigs," Blake thought back. He was getting proud of himself. Luke wondered if Blake knew the trouble he was in, and that made him worry. *Lose one worry and gain another. Blake was fine, and we can communicate, so please, Blake, be smart for me.*

"I love you," Luke shot back. All of a sudden he had forgotten his mission and only wanted his brother safe. "Ellie, are you okay? Blake and I are fine." Each time Luke did this, he concentrated with all his might. It was such an effort that he felt his head ache.

"Good," was all the response Luke received. He guessed that had to do.

It seemed to take forever. The reeds were cutting into their hands as they moved them aside. Those behind had to wipe off the blood from the trees and grasses, so as not to leave a trace. The push forward continued in silence until the bruised and tired group could smell the salt air of the sound. Because they were holding their breath as much as they could, they could also hear the water gently slap the shore as the sound sat calmly waiting for its riders.

Reaching the shore first was Wematin, then Sooleawa. The children climbed into their respective boats, and when they held out their hands to the settlers to come aboard, the tense air around the canoes relaxed, and the travelers were sure-footed and quick.

Several of the groups were in an area far down the bank from the boats, and Manteo could see by the sliver of a moon their black masses huddled in the reeds. Boats were manned, and the exchange of paddles and loading of people began to happen. The sounds were very far away now, and if they could shove off and get a good ways into the water before dawn, they had a chance of not being seen.

This time the colonial men took to the paddles to give the Indians a rest. These Indians had extracted them from harm, and the colonial men wanted to show gratitude to the men who came to their aid. It seemed that both sets of people knew that a connection was about to happen. Connections were sometimes not smooth, and language was a problem, as was hierarchy. Would the colonists take direction from a woman? On the other side, the Indians thought, do they have enough people to start all over again and make a colony of their own? Or would they elect to live among the natives? All was going through the minds of the men who rowed and the men who watched. The women also recognized that life would once again be different, maybe even difficult. But eventually they must adjust to the new land.

After a mentally stressful though uneventful crossing, the sun was just beginning to show its head behind the trees and hills of Hatteras

Island. The Indians at the front of each boat slipped overboard and began dragging the loaded canoes toward shore. Some other Indians jumped over and reached in to lift out supplies and baggage. There were also weapons—a couple of muskets, a few swords—and smaller items. One brave had an armful of swords, and one of them slipped and cut his arm. He dropped the bunch, uttering cross words and retrieving them in a better grip. In his haste, he left one, and as the passengers departing the boats stirred the bottom, the mud finally took the prize.

Most of the men walking the canoes to the shore were now naked to the waist, with only the hide strip crisscrossing their chests. They had removed the uncomfortable breastplates and left them stacked in the middle of the canoes. The laces around their boots and pants glistened as they floated on the water, chasing the men who walked the boat through the marsh grass. The Croatoan were still painted for battle, or camouflage—it was hard to tell which. The familiar faces of the week before had been transformed into masks of strangers who would do battle in the night. They truly had not wanted to lose any of their own people trying to save others, so their plan involved the need to slip away from the enemy. They were successful. The enemy was not spotted, only heard. The conjuror of the tribe, Sucki (meaning black), had read the fires, picked the time, named the braves, and determined the best trail to the stockade, even though he actually had no knowledge of Roanoke Island's landscape. Sucki was sure of his plan. This night he gained stature, although later he would lose it.

They were all glad, but cautious. What if this was a personal thing to the Roanoke Indians, and what if they believed that even one of these fugitives had offended them? They would not take this development in a friendly manner. War was a possibility, but Manteo felt that the colonials would be a help in battle, as they were better equipped than the enemy. Even four guns were better than none, and he had counted at least ten. But this was all a guess. Maybe they had already exacted their revenge. Maybe beheading some of the colonials was enough for the Roanoke chief.

One by one the settlers disembarked from each of the seven canoes. Some were dressed in colonial attire, some with deerskin shirts, and others in heavy, shabby shirts of the day. The canoes were being dragged from the water and tied with a reed rope to stakes in the ground. The woman holding the baby began to step out of the canoe, helped by a very frail-looking Englishman. She was holding the baby tight, but she slipped. There was a collective gasp, and an Indian in the boat threw down his paddle and caught her before her second foot even got wet. The child whimpered, and immediately in that moment she was the center of attention.

Light hit the face under the blanket. With blond curls, a pair of clear blue eyes was peeking from behind the thick cloth cover, and the Indians stared at the child they had rescued. Most of the braves had not had the contact with the English that Manteo had experienced. But they knew of his journeys and his connection to these people. And because of his having seen worlds they would never see—and his position in the tribe—they had great respect for him. If he said these strangers were to be protected, then protected they would be.

As the Indians, colonists, and three children of the future began their trek to the village, the tired company had a relaxed and happy feeling. One of the colonists put his hand on Luke's shoulder and said simply, "Thank you. If you have been shipwrecked, we will take care of you. You have helped save us, and we will not forget."

Luke looked up at Manteo, and Manteo gave him a wink. They both seemed to be of the mind that the shipwreck story was a good one, and they would not try to explain anything else. It made them both feel less anxious. They need not otherwise explain three obviously English children, dressed from head to toe in Indian style, greeting them at the fort.

As the party collected their belongings and followed each other, they were aware of the still fresh danger of being caught up in an Indian war on their behalf. Several of the Indian braves stayed behind to hide the canoes and to eliminate the signs of a landing. If they covered the scene with bushes and reeds, it would be obvious—as time went by and the green foliage began to turn brown—where exactly the craft had been hidden. So the braves started one by one lifting the canoes to a wooded area unseen from the water. They placed the boats under living ferns that grew tall and could easily conceal the craft. Once the boats were safely out of sight, the men joined the others, almost walking backward to check to see if they had been followed. So far, nothing.

The path from the sound was well worn, as the Croatoan usually hunted across the sound on the mainland for larger game, as well as to spare the game on the island. They also liked spending time on a hunt, especially anticipating its conclusion. That was time for a feast. On those occasions, celebration and feasting began before storing and preparing the food for winter.

This path was also hidden from the sound, and the Indians led the colonists in a wide rather than narrow line away from the shore, toward the trees, until the path appeared. It was amazing both to the settlers and children how aware the tribe was. Living in a natural state, one learned many things and became acquainted with everything around them.

As they walked the path, the settlers began to talk among themselves. It was the first time they had felt comfortable enough to interact and check with their companions as to their well-being. They found that they all had weathered the rescue with only cuts and bruises, and maybe some were a bit sore from all that crawling. The one colonist who had spoken to Luke explained to the others that the children had been shipwrecked and the Indians were taking care of them. Ellie heard this and smiled.

Did Luke tell them that? she wondered. *He is a lot smarter than I thought. I would never have come up with an explanation like that.* Actually Ellie had wondered how to explain her presence and was a little nervous about what she would say if someone inquired. She fired off a thought to Luke: "I think you are smart!"

Luke turned around and gave her a funny look.

Ellie and Luke both began thinking thoughts along the same line. *Why is this happening to us? How is this to be explained?* Ellie was going over and over in her mind about what Weroansqua had told her. And ahead of her, Luke was thinking, *I have always wondered how I know where Ellie and Blake are and when they are coming. I just thought it was because we lived together. I did not know we could do this.* Ellie was thinking that the first chance they were all together, she would tell them what Weroansqua said. Ellie had not had time before the rescue.

After what seemed a long time, the group came upon a number of crop fields. Breathing a sweet smell they all worked their way through the tall stalks of dried corn at the edge of the village. Farther along, the trees had been cut, and the fields had been burned to create an excellent space for the village gardens and to add to the richness of the soil for the following year of planting. Finally they came upon the circle of longhouses nestled among the trees. Although the trees partially hid the houses, the travelers soon entered a huge clearing with a blazing fire pit. The whole group welcomed the warmth of the fire. Everyone was wet from sweat, worry, sound water, and mud. The fire in the compound must have been started at daybreak, in anticipation of the group coming home safely.

Each lead Indian took his party to one of the reed-covered enclosures of a longhouse. The Indian women were there to help the settlers unload their bundles and eat. They devoured the corn cakes and mash that the women had prepared. The fresh water from the spring probably was the most welcomed of anything they had. They ate their fill, and the women of the tribe indicated to them that they should rest, motioning toward the fur-covered platforms. At that, they left the tired travelers alone in the huge houses and went about their daily chores.

★ 11 ★

The Gift

The colonists slept peacefully for the first time in a very long time. Life at the fort was tense and stressful since the beheading of their friends. Beheading was such a primitive killing and so cruel. They wondered who would be next. Every night they questioned if this would be their last. They had many discussions about it, and there was no joy in their existence. The pressure of what to do depended on a rescue from England, and that looked like, if it came, it would be too late. It was as if their grand experiment for the Queen was a forgotten one, and they had been thrown away.

There was no answer they could think of, and they certainly did not think of this one. As each awakened, fresh food and water were at their side so that they could renew their bodies and sleep again. They did not see the maidens coming and going with fresh clothes, nourishment, and quiet. In the late afternoon, some began to wander out of the longhouses where they were staying and walk around the compound, with only occasional glances from the Indians. As each woke from sleep, they put on the fresh tunics and deer-hide pants or leggings and emerged to see what was happening. Did they dream it all? Were they really safe? Could this nightmare be over? All these questions were foremost in their minds. They indicated in a secret and hurried place, to anyone who discovered the empty fort, where they could be found, but now there was no anxiety for the next minute. They were safe to wait and live peacefully until they could begin again, or until their ships came back from England. Should their ships arrive, they knew what signs to look for, and the colonials had completed that task. They gathered at the side of the clearing to make a plan for their lives.

The men and women talked, while the English and Indian children seemed to be making friends, with Luke's efforts. As the groups relaxed, it did not take long for friendships to develop among those of like ages. Blake had his little band of men, and he was showing them the camp. He gained the respect of the Indian boys earlier with his ability to catch on to knife throwing with Wematin. He practiced daily, and with Wematin's help, there were contests, to the delight of the children, who certainly would rather play with the English boy than do the chores set out for them. As a result of Wematin working so hard with Blake, the other braves, who were fathers, began to take more time with their own boys, in hopes of equaling the skill of the little English boy and his mentor. It was always friendly competition, which usually ended with Wematin in a wrestling match with another young brave. The talk of war was over, and temporarily they all settled into a more peaceful existence.

Each of the English "stowaways" was available for translating, so the settlers were able to have their questions answered and anxieties calmed. They began to enjoy life again.

Blake took his little group to see the wolf carver. They all sat around his hut and watched as the old man took a chunk of wood and, with great skill and only a crude knife, revealed the wolf hidden in the middle of the block of wood. It seemed that he chipped away every small shaving of wood that was not the wolf until the head, body, feet, and tail were revealed. Each English child got one, but the one that Blake received was of a different piece of wood—much darker, and with more detail than the others. The children were satisfied, and they moved on to the tree structures and vine bridges that made up the refuge part of the village. Blake's tour ended with an exploration of the caves that were carved out of the hill, leading down to either the mouth of the stream or the grotto at the other end.

The stream was wide and deep enough for a canoe, but in places it was more shallow, so walking was the best way to see the underground water-way. The children followed all the way to the waterfall that ran off from the huge gusher above. Shards of light entered in places where the stream neared the top of the falls. The water ran from the gusher that was being pushed up from the earth's floor, down through a winding path near the bottom of the hill, and on to the sound, where it emptied its fresh water into the salt water of the sound. There was just enough current in the quiet water to keep it fresh, and mostly the tribe used the stream near the end of its run for bathing. At the runoff the women also had their washing area, as well as a spot where they beat the hides to soften them.

The braves collected large boulders from across the sound and carried them to the island to put at the site to help the women. A lot of activity took place near the runoff, and rocks from a riverbed on the mainland were stacked in a pile for the settler women to use against the boulders. On their way back to the grotto, they met the women of the tribe on a similar walk, motioning to the settlers where they could wash up and clean their clothes.

As the colonists were learning the lay of the land, Manteo also was in the business of tour guide, but his motives were not as social as the others. His task was showing the settlers where to hide in case their escape had not been as successful as it seemed. The men were shown where to hide, where to stand and fight, and where to stow their muskets and tools of protection for easy access. As the men learned of the rope bridges, tree platforms, and rooms hidden from view, they began to hatch a plan of their own.

They inquired of Manteo if there was another area such as this one, where they could construct their own compound—with the secret places and protection the Indians had, but where they could live as they were taught. They had learned quite a lot about living out in the open, with no place to get away from an enemy. They had only been in Manteo's charge for twenty-four hours, and they knew what a sacrifice the Indians were making by having to share their quarters, food, water, and clothes with so many people. They did not want to be a burden on their benefactors, so they wanted a place of their own.

After that, the exploration expeditions took place every day. First one, then another brave would take the men to look for the proper setting for their colony. It was not possible for Manteo to accompany them every time, but when they got back, they would sit with him and discuss their findings. Manteo, with his lad, Luke, would listen to the colonists talk about their hopes and dreams. They developed a plan to help the colonials settle on the Croatoan land. Everyone decided to proceed with all speed to accomplish the task, and braves were spared each day to help hasten the project. Knowing that they once again would be self-sufficient, the colonials began to smile more, taking an interest in everything the tribe did and sharing knowledge of the others' skills.

The Indian women took time to help the anxious women of the settlement relax by engaging them in sharing cooking chores, gardening duties, and preserving the foods that had already been harvested, and—most hilarious of all—teaching the settlers to fish. Colonials had begun learning to be hunters and gatherers as a way of life. They were quite well adjusted to hunting, but fishing did not come as naturally, and as the Roanoke Indians shared their bounty from the sound, they were just beginning to teach the colonials to gather fish in nets and by spear. Then a conflict arose between the two societies of people, and the Roanoke turned against them. Fishing was still a new skill, one the colonials had not yet learned. As the Croatoan reintroduced the use of nets, for gathering multiple fish, even though the colonials had mastered the art of *making* the nets, they were not yet sure how to anchor them in the sound in a position to catch the fish. The children watched as the colonials tried to pull in the nets without losing all the fish before they got to shore, or to the canoe, if they were farther off shore.

Ellie busied herself by taking care of the English child Virginia. She had great fun playing with the little girl, and it freed her mother, Eleanor, to learn along with the other women. Eleanor was fascinated by the knowledge that Ellie's given name was the same as hers, but thought nothing of it as it was a common English name, and many girls back in England also bore that name. Ellie was a little disappointed not to be spending her days with Sooleawa, but she was included in all the discussions at night around the small fire in the longhouse. She loved listening to the plans for the wedding, the gowns, the headdresses—all the stuff girls talk about when they are about to be married. Fires were kept burning in most of the houses—not large fires, but just large enough to keep away the pesky mosquitoes and green flies that could do much damage if one forgot to protect against them.

At night in Weroansqua's house, the talk centered around Sooleawa's upcoming wedding to Keme (meaning thunder). The tasks of the older women were on a much grander scale that those of the young maidens. The women needed to plan the festival, which was to be a grand affair. Keme had been named as a child after a year of observation because he became so excited when the thunder cracked. He seemed to want to get near it rather than away from it. The choice was whether to name him Kitchi (meaning brave) or Keme. They had decided on Thunder, as he was both bold and brave. The preparations were to include inviting the two closest tribes on the island: the Hatorask and the Kinnakeet. When a chief's daughter married, the celebration was of great importance. The festival would last for days. Besides the wedding, competitive games among the tribes were scheduled, and food from all corners as well as tribal dancing were also much anticipated. A lot had to be done.

Weroansqua also had another task to perform. The visit with the three English children was coming to a close, as she knew from her meetings with Powwaw. The old shaman was most concerned about Ellie finding her way after the stay with the tribe was complete. He pressured Weroansqua—he was insistent—to have her private time with Ellie and the boys. So, one night, Weroansqua instructed Manteo, Wematin, Loutau, and Sooleawa to go to another place while she and Powwaw lit the fire and confronted the spirits. Manteo and the others did not understand, but he never contradicted his mother. Manteo took everyone to one of the refuge spots, giving the chief and the priest their time alone.

Luke, Ellie, and Blake were a little surprised by this meeting with the chief and the priest, but they suspected what was going to happen. After all, they had experienced the strangeness of their being on the rescue, and they had been so busy with the settlers and their position as mentors to them that they had discussed their departure only a little. On the first night after the rescue, Ellie had moved her sleeping spot near the boys and began to whisper while others were asleep, tired from all their efforts to live both their lives and the lives of the strangers. Tribal cultures take being the host seriously. They did not know that the great Weroansqua was awake and smiling.

"Blake, you know that I wanted to talk to you when we were at the stockade, but there was so much going on, it didn't seem to be the right time. Did you get a message in your mind from either me or Luke?" whispered Ellie.

"I know how to do that, too. I have done it before, when we were at home, but I thought it was an accident. I thought a message to Luke, and I tried hard in my mind to have him hear it, and he did," said Blake.

Luke answered, "Okay, we all have that gift, and we know that now. But Ellie, you know more than we do because you said Weroansqua told you." Luke now had his head between the younger ones, as he positioned himself to a whispering position that would allow all of them to speak quietly without waking the others.

"We are descendants of this tribe through Grandmom, Weroansqua said, and my mother, Annie, had a gift that she was not strong enough to use, so she gave her gifts to me when she died.

"My gifts are two instead of one. I think that's how it goes. I didn't ask many questions, because I had to think about it, and I didn't understand it until the rescue and I tried it." Ellie was whispering to both boys, as she switched around to be heard. Both were paying attention. "Before I could say anything to you, we left for the rescue. She said Grandmom has the gift, too, because she is directly from this tribe. And I have it from my mother, and you both have it from Aunt Nett. But I don't think Aunt Nett had as much in her blood as my mother, so she is not exactly like us. But Weroansqua said that Aunt Nett passed strong blood to both of you, so we are all three carriers of this gift. I'm not really sure what it is, but I'm going to ask."

"What kind of gift do you *guess* it is?" Blake was the one with all the questions. Even though Luke wanted to know also, Blake beat him to the punch.

"I don't know," said Ellie, "but together we should ask. There never seems to be a good time, because there is so much going on, and sometimes I forget."

"We will ask tomorrow," said Luke, "so don't forget. Tomorrow is the day. And I think we are going home soon. Powwaw sort of said so the other day."

They all agreed that no matter what they were assigned to do on the following day, one of them would sneak in to speak to Weroansqua. Ellie wriggled back to her sleeping spot and fell fast asleep, as her mind wandered into a dream of an adventure with her wolf.

The next day, Blake left his admirers watching Mingan carving wolves and walked back to the longhouse. He walked in, looked around, and found Weroansqua busy chewing on a deer hide to make it soft. He stood beside her silently and watched. She turned to him and motioned for him to sit. As he watched the stately chief doing menial work, he thought of how he might communicate to her what he wanted, and the answer came back.

"Tonight."

Blake's eyes widened as he realized he had wanted to speak but did not know the words. His mind had connected, though, as had hers. She reached down, took his head in her hands, and pulled him forward for a kiss on the forehead. Then, with her hand, palm down, she motioned for him to go back to what he was doing. Blake slowly got up and started to walk away. He then turned back and put his arms around the old woman's back and gave her a hug. Now, this was as big a shock to Weroansqua as the shock was to Blake when she seemed to speak to him. Indians did not put their hand on their chief. This little English boy was truly her own, and she would be sad to see him go.

Blake reached the entrance of the longhouse, stood, and searched the compound for either Luke or Ellie. He spied Luke practicing his whip, knowing there were contests at the wedding, and if there were ones for kids, Luke wanted to make Manteo proud. Blake started to run, then thought better of it. He quickly walked to the place where Luke was beginning to crack the braided strips of thin rawhide that Manteo had made for his whip.

"I asked her," he said, with satisfaction of being the first.

"What?" Luke concentrated on another throw to make a sound.

"I asked Weroansqua if she would talk to us about our gifts," Blake said.

"And when did you learn to speak the language?" Luke inquired.

"Well, I didn't actually ask," he said. "I sort of was thinking of how to ask when she sort of answered."

"Yeah?" Luke was skeptical. "What did she say?" He was grinning, not expecting an answer, and certainly not the one he got.

"She didn't say anything. She thought me an answer, and she said she wanted to talk to us." Blake was now getting confused at how to even get this across to his older brother and not sound like a nitwit.

Luke was still a little puzzled at their conversation, when Manteo walked over and sat on a log nearby.

"The chief and the shaman will talk to you and Ellie tonight after the meal," he said simply. Then he got up and calmly walked away, taking great strides to get back to what he was doing across the yard.

Luke and Blake stared at each other, and both hearts skipped a beat at the same time.

"We need to tell Ellie," they agreed.

Ellie already knew. Weroansqua had indicated it to her when she approached the chief earlier in the morning. She knew that Luke would be spending time with Powwaw today, and she assumed he would tell him. Luke did go to see Powwaw that day, after he, Blake, and Manteo had spoken. He was surprised when it was not a usual day of looking for strange healing things, but Powwaw was in full paint and dressed in a white deer hide that had been beaten and bleached in the sun with the strong potions Powwaw had at his ready.

"We will eat together tonight in the chief's lodge," he communicated to Luke. He did not speak, nor did he signal anything. He was very proudly watching the gift work on his little friend.

Then it was time. Manteo, Sooleawa, Wematin, and Loutau, Weroansqua's brother, left the lodge to eat at the communal fire in the middle of the village. The three children were left in the presence of Weroansqua and Powwaw, both in high ceremonial robes, and the beautiful white wolf—the one they had seen on the first night. Sitting on a high perch, seemingly made for him, was a large black raven. His eyes were so clear, they were mirrors. The meal was served by several of the young Indian maidens. They, too, were dressed in nearly white tunics, and their eyes were covered by masks, with only slits cut for vision. It was a special meal, some of which Powwaw had prepared, and it was served in a special way. The food was good, but it was different, and as the children ate, the food and special drink began to take hold. They seemed to get very drowsy, and Ellie put her head on Luke's shoulder. He in turn cuddled Blake to him, and the three of them drifted into another consciousness. Powwaw's drink had been special and particular. It would eliminate the need for words and leave only thoughts for communication. He began,

"Our chief, Weroansqua, informed Ellie of a few of her gifts, but this is the time for all of you to know who you are to us, and who you are to yourselves. You have the blood of the wolf and the blood of Weroansqua coursing through your veins. The wolf's blood is ancient. Before this island was with people, when only the wolf was here, we think the wolf came from the great ocean, from a land that disappeared under the sea near Dawnland, long before time began. He brought man and began our tribe. The spirit of the wolf transferred to Weroansqua when she was born, and the wolf has watched over her all her life. You are also being protected by the wolf. You are of a special tribe. Your grandmother in your life is the carrier. She is a direct descendant of this tribe. The coming child of Sooleawa will marry an Englishman, whose family name is Jennette. From the child's loins will spring a child who will pass on the spirit of Weroansqua to her children, and their children who come after her. This bold heart is shared with your grandmother and was especially strong in her daughter, Annie—your mother, Ellie. The heart was so strong that Annie could not live with it, and it was passed to you, her daughter. Luke and Blake, your mother, Jeanette, passed the same blood on to you, but for her, she was only a carrier. She did not receive the gifts for herself. She could only pass them on to you. Your mother will not understand this part of you, but your grandmother will. Any wonder you may have, your grandmother will be given the answer.

"You all are watched over by three spirits from this tribe, ones who were chosen to guide you. Ellie, the name of your spirit guide is Travis. Luke, your guide is Micah. And Blake, your guide is Brendan. They are the ones who brought you here through a passage called a time portal that only they know. They will bring you back one more time, when Weroansqua is dying, so that all knowledge will pass from her as she takes her last breath. You all have gifts, but they are not the same. All of you can communicate with each other by thought. In the presence of Ellie, all of you have the power to move objects, but only with the concentration of the three of you. Ellie, you are the only one who can communicate with the fish of the ocean, the fowl of the air, and the creatures who walk the earth. You have the powers of Weroansqua.

"These gifts are only given to you as long as your spirit is good. When you use the gifts for evil, they will be taken away. Your hearts are pure and will remain so as long as you possess these powers. Your spirit guides are here in this place. They are with you all the time. There is one more thing. You are of the tribe of the wolf. The wolf is strong and wise. He is compassionate and generous with his pack, and he is loyal and a protector of those with whom he connects. You have seen the wolves following your movements, and they always will. They are connected to your spirit guides and will never allow you to be in grave danger. The full moon in the coldest time is the moon of the wolf. On that night, and that night only, you may play with your wolves. You will know when.

"You will be able to recognize in several ways when your spirit is near. There might be a sudden change of temperature in the room—either warm air or a warm glow. You can smell an unusual aroma in your presence, or you might see light shafts shooting across the room. These are signs. Sometimes you will hear your name whispered when no one else is around. Listen at those times, and think. Any time you see white sparkles or flashes of white, your spirit is trying to get your attention. You must learn to listen to your inside voices. Do not worry about your dreams. They do not come to you without purpose. You do not wake up from a dream. The dream wakes you up. Take a few minutes to think about them, because they are messages, I might even send you a message, and I would like for you to know that I, too, will always be with you.

"As I said, you all have a wolf watching over you. They are mighty creatures. They have a sense of smell that is one hundred times that of a human. If you are in trouble, they will smell it and come to you. They are different from other animals. They do not fight for dominance as other animals do. They only display a superior attitude. Ellie, when you are attacked in spirit by others, your attitude protects you. It is an inner confidence that all is well that saves you. Know the wolf, as he has the ability to blend in to avoid trouble. That is why you only see a shadow. They are aware at all times of danger to themselves and to you, and they will not show themselves until they are needed. Ellie, the name of your wolf is Twylah. Blake, yours is named Theo. And Luke, yours is Rafe. He is the wisest of the wolves, as you are also wise.

"The most important thing you will bring away from this night is greater knowledge of your ability to communicate with each other. Even your grandmother does not have that, but she knows that you do. We communicate to your grandmother through her dreams. Don't be surprised if she knows what you are thinking. It is because we told her."

The children slept soundly until the next morning, and they awakened to find Manteo and Wematin standing over them for another lesson. They quickly got the boys fed and out to the secret training spot. The contests among the three tribes would not be lost for the Croatoans, not on their own territory. They would make sure of that. It was also fun for the boys to watch Manteo and Wematin compete, Wematin having been taught by Manteo. It was no surprise that the strapping younger brave could best the mightier brave, but only half the time.

What time was not spent preparing for the upcoming festival was spent helping the men of the new colony construct their houses in the area that had been given to them. The Indians learned much from the colonial men, and they in turn marveled at the skill of the Indians. The colonials especially learned how to turn natural things into useful items. They learned how to use the forest. Rope was made from vines, reeds and small saplings were used for construction, and with the tools of the English, many more tubs and craters were created for washing, carrying, making dyes, crushing corn, and storage. All the while, guards were stationed near the sound and the outskirts of Croatoa in anticipation of a possible retaliation from the Roanoke tribe. It never came.

The colonials chose an area south of the Croatoan in the trees, on high ground, more near the sea than the sound. The colonial men worked tirelessly to remove the burden of their numbers from the friendly and generous Indians. The women did their best to help, but because construction was such hard work, they spent most of their time learning how to soften hides, make clothing, cook what they had, prepare a garden for themselves, and of course help with the upcoming wedding. They were as excited as the Indians and had many ideas. Virginia became so close to Ellie that they acted like sisters. There was much affection between them, and Eleanor could also talk to Ellie. Eleanor was amazed at how satisfying it was to sit down with a ten-year-old and learn so many things.

One morning Manteo and Wematin awakened Luke and Blake before daybreak. When they dressed and came outside, several groups of Indians and settlers were waiting and busying themselves with weapons. Luke and Blake were wide-eyed at the sight, just knowing they were going to war. But where was the war paint? Why were they not given armor? Everybody looked so happy, and the women were fixing a big breakfast around the communal fire of quail eggs, corn cakes, and oysters. This did not look like the earlier war party.

"We are going on a hunt, across to the mainland," said Manteo. "We are going to need much meat and fowl, and we are going to show both you and our friends the shell midden that is nearest to us in the sound."

"What is a shell midden?" Luke finally beat Blake to a question, and Blake clenched his fists, pulled up his shoulders, and brought them down hard in a motion of frustration.

Luke smiled. He had seen that look of disgust before, usually leading up to a small temper tantrum, but Blake did not go that far this time.

"It is a place where we and others before us have dumped our shells, bones, and things no longer useful. Ours is a big one, used for so many years that it is itself an island. We will find shells to use for decoration, bones for our vests, and many things that you will like. First we will go over to the mainland to hunt. We need much food for the festivities, as we have invited many people."

The men and boys boarded the canoes and set off for a trip across the water to better and more luscious hunting than their own island provided. Most of the tribes respected the frailty of the land and did not want to overuse the island, which would prevent others from feeding.

It took them until noon to reach their destination, and another hour to ready themselves for the hunt. It became obvious that this was going to be an all-day, all-night affair. The Indians began to scout the ground for signs of deer, wild hogs, and the occasional bear. They read the ground as if it were written. Some squirrels were shot, and a few rabbits, the English marveling at the skill their new friends had with the bow. The larger game remained to be brought down. Finally they came upon a pile of fresh dung that was a size comparable to a deer's. The settlers did not try to interrupt the Indians, and they learned much. Each broken twig, twisted limb, dung heap, and piece of trampled grass led them to their prey. Most important was to follow the two deep ruts in the ground that indicated the hooves of a deer. They could tell the deer's size by the depth of the rut.

After an hour and a half, they spotted the animal, grazing in an open clearing, and the shot was given to Wematin. He was known to be good with the bow and arrow, and they did not want to miss the first shot. Wematin pulled back the gut of his bow and let the arrow fly. The big buck fell to the ground with such a thud that the birds left their perches in the trees and flew away. The other braves rushed to the fallen animal to check his wound. They did not want the animal to suffer, nor did they want him to get up. It was a shot to the heart. The deer had turned with the sound, his front was to Wematin, and it was an excellent kill. He was skinned and dressed right on the spot, which made for easy carrying and fresher meat. The excess was buried. It would not do to leave rotting meat in the forest. They found a spot under the trees, dug a hole in the cool earth, wrapped the meat and hide tightly, and marked the spot in order to come back to it after the hunt was done.

They started out again, and this time it was decided that Keme would be allowed to fall the next animal, no matter what it was. Keme was anxious. It was necessary for him to prove that he would be a good provider, and he needed to do this in front of Manteo. Keme was secretly hoping for a bear, so he concentrated his scouting on signs that would indicate bear territory. Another deer was sighted, and Keme gave his turn to Matunaaga (meaning one who fights), and his aim was also true. Keme and the group continued to look for a bear. Meanwhile, they collected several turkeys, duck, geese, and a huge hog that wandered into their sight after another turkey.

Finally, near dark, they came upon a bear sign. From the paw prints it was large and male. They followed cautiously, as this animal was one that would fight back rather than run away. At long last they heard the crushing of bushes and brush that could only be the sought-after creature. Keme got ready, and the others did also, as killing a bear often required backup. Several of the braves readied their bows, as it might take more than one arrow to fell such a creature. There would be no time if it was just wounded to get another arrow in position for a second shot. There needed to be several already in hand to fire fast.

The huge animal came in sight. He was burrowing around a pile of broken limbs and logs that appeared to be infested with bees. Another problem. This kill had to be quick, and it had to be correct. The bear was not looking, nor did he smell the intruders, because they were downwind of him. Keme readied his bow and let fly. His arrow found its mark, high on the neck. Keme had aimed toward the jugular vein, a sure-kill shot. The huge bear flinched and stood up to swat the arrow out of his neck. At that time all the other arrows flew in unison, and the bear turned, found his attackers, and lunged toward them. Manteo pushed Luke up a tree, and Wematin did the same for Blake. They climbed as high as they could, praying all the while that nobody got hurt. The bear charged. Luke and Blake could see the entire scene. As the bear began to stumble forward, it had turned, showing his underbelly, and Keme got off his second shot. This time it found the heart. He was done. The loudest cheer ricocheted through the forest. It was a shout of many tired men, giving off all that energy they used before to be quiet—a thunderous sound of success!

The worn-out hunters made their way back to the canoes with their treasures. Wouldn't this be the greatest celebration, especially when the women found that the warriors also brought back honey in the washed and stitched-up stomach bags of the animals they had dressed? The hunters slept in their canoes with their fresh meat in the cool water and waited for the dawn. They would stop at the shell midden on the way back. This was the most exciting day the boys had ever had.

The shell midden was a surprise. It was a mountain of shells, bones, and carcasses. Here birds dropped scallop, oyster, or clam shells on the huge pile to break them open, allowing them to get to the meat. The Indians crawled around the mound, which was as big as another island. The midden was even then hundreds of years old. Animals, birds, and humans had deposited their waste on this spot, which over the years all melded together to form a massive rock. Here and there were small trees and bushes seeming to grow from the rock, planted there by birds dropping seeds. The company collected beautiful shells—even pearls in the broken oysters—and bones that could be colored and strung for body decoration. Everywhere was a treasure to be found, too much to bring home. This was truly a special sight. The seagulls squawked and cawed at the intrusion, flying around screaming at the trespassers to go away. They did, but not without absolutely the most gorgeous empty shells and bones that Luke and Blake had ever seen. This was going to be a beautiful festival, and the Croatoan were going to outshine the other tribes.

Keme was the most excited of all. He already had bear claws strung around his neck.

★ 12 ★

The Wedding Festival

Upon returning from the hunt, the work was only partially finished. The women took over storing the treasures, and the men began again. Breaks in the nets needed mending in preparation for catching many fish. Shells weighted down the sides and corners of the nets to ensure a wide cast to bring in the large amounts of fish trapped in that circle. It was necessary to farm many turtles, as delicious turtle soup was a delicacy. Their shells also made great rattles to be used in the dance. The diamondback terrapin was the most sought after. They set about to collect as many oysters, clams, and scallops as the men could dig in the beds they had created, located in secret places of the sound. A collection of spears was made with slim poles tipped by the tail of the horseshoe crab and limbs whittled to killing points. The fishermen rowed out to sink fish traps that would be checked daily. These traps caught many things: crabs, fish, small octopi, and sometimes a skate, which made great steaks.

Mingan switched his attention from wolves to carving spoons from wood and shell. They hollowed out the gourds they had been growing to provide drinking vessels, and also used them to fashion rattles for the dance. Many of the women busied themselves making baskets from grasses and reeds treated and woven in ornate designs. The smaller baskets would be given as gifts to the guests, and the larger ones served as containers to display food to be consumed once the other tribes arrived. Elaborate designs and colors indicated the Croatoans' specific style. Drink was fermented, and yaupon leaves treated and boiled for tea, with stronger potions for the men. The activity was endless, yet so relaxing to everyone after the stress and anticipation of war. A portion of honey from the hunt was given to Powwaw to brew in a special ceremonial toast.

The camp was alive with people contributing to the separate duties that served to make a grand impression on the other two tribes. The settlers tried to help, but preoccupation with building their own village took up most of their time. Their activity, though, did get them out of the way so that the Indians could do what they knew had to be done. The newly arrived company did not want the inconvenience of their numbers to get in the way of their benefactors' work. All thoughts of self were abandoned, as the colonials tried at this time to repay the debt they felt they owed to Manteo. The women of the settlement participated in making reed mats for the guests to sit on and scraping the deer hide with some of the sharper shells gathered at the midden. Clothing was an important part of everyone's plan. Even the settlers wanted the Croatoan to outshine any visitor from another tribe.

The most important thing for the women of the settlement was to help make the wedding tunic for Sooleawa. Bleaching out deer hide and constructing this beautiful garment didn't even seem like work to them. At night around various campfires, women sat in groups stitching patterns with shells, dying shells and bones, and creating accessories that the Croatoan women possibly had never seen. They tore apart things they had saved from the Roanoke Island encampment in order to present a garment that was unique. It was also important both to the women of the tribe and the settlement that the dress be a surprise, and having it done by the colonials allowed the secret to be kept away from prying eyes.

The maidens of the tribe also wanted to be a part of the wedding dress. Sooleawa was their friend, and they relished the opportunity to show their affection. They visited the camps of the English women and bonded over the tunic. The wedding was healing the wounds in the hearts of the displaced colonial women and allowing the young Indian maidens a glimpse into how other people designed and crafted garments. The tribe was benefiting greatly, as were the settlers. It was not unusual for fits of laughter to drift through the camps. Sooleawa was a little jealous that she could not be part of the fun, but she understood it was all for her, so she spent a lot of time with Ellie and Virginia.

Every single bird brought back to the camp was carefully plucked for its gorgeous feathers. The most beautiful of the feathers were always the ones underneath, those not seen at first glance when the bird was in flight. The women had never seen such vivid blues, greens, shades of yellow and turquoise, and varying reds beneath the outer layers of darker, more drab feathers. Hair ornaments made from feathers and shells were the specialty of a few of the tribeswomen, and they carefully put them together and stored them in the colonial area in anticipation of the ceremony.

Probably the most outstanding piece of jewelry was made for Weroansqua. There was no jewelry for the bride, as her beauty was supposed to shine from within. The much-admired creation for Weroansqua was a necklace made of glass beads from the colonials and included pearls, iridescent shells, bleached strips of hide, and tufts of a rare white rabbit hide saved for this occasion. It was like a collar that sat on the base of the neck and covered her entire neck to just under the chin. Nobody had ever seen such a piece, not in this area of the world. It was the most extravagant thing the colonial women had ever crafted. The necklace held the hearts of those who designed it, and it was the most magnificent adornment even they had ever seen, much less had a hand in making. They had tears in their eyes as they presented it to Weroansqua. At first she wanted it for Sooleawa, but tradition would not allow it, and it would have been less than gracious for her to refuse such a special piece. It was appropriate for a queen, and at this point, Weroansqua was their queen.

It also fell to the settlers to create a headpiece for her. They matched the necklace as much as possible, and the two together were not to be believed. One of the women donated a mirror to be cut into small circles and placed on the headpiece. This contribution came at a great sacrifice to everyone, as mirrors were prized possessions. The tiny lights danced from all angles and truly gave Weroansqua a royal appearance.

Excited to quit working on their camp and curious for an adventure, the colonial men left to accompany the braves on a trip to the ocean. Here lived huge, mighty turtles; shark, which had the most supple skin for drums; porpoises; and large ocean shells. Great swimmers and even better divers, the braves delighted in diving into the deepest spots to bring up coral and shells that lived only in the ocean. They also needed the largest whelks for horns, and a festival of this caliber needed lots of trumpet flourishes, both for the games and the ceremony.

The most dangerous part of the hunt was that for the right whale, which at this time was migrating down the coast to warmer breeding grounds. One unusual habit of this particular whale was its love of swimming near the beach. It was prized for oil and blubber used in cooking and glistening the dark skin of Indians. Its blubber was also used for soap, making candles, and fuel for soaking hides that would be wrapped around the thick poles used as torches. The bones prized by primitive groups for their sturdiness served to make strong tools, hammers, cutting blades, heavy clubs, and musical instruments. The old carver begged to be given an amount of bone for carving out dolphin images and wolf designs, also used as gifts. Only the bravest and most skilled went after this leviathan, the most splendid mammal of them all. Indians were no strangers to whaling in those days, as whales were numerous before the English came.

Of course, much attention was paid to the beauty of the ceremony itself and the feast for the guests, but other things needed to be considered.

The men—with all the hunting, fishing, building, carving of bowls, and providing shelter for a several-day event—were in their spare time, if there was any, practicing their skills for the games. Luke and Blake were both excited about competing along with the other Indian boys in knife throwing, hatchet throwing, and whip skills, as well as wrestling, foot races, balance, and marksmanship. There was even to be storytelling, and all the tribes looked forward to that. It was one of the most anticipated events for the children. The elders could weave great stories, and new tales to surprise and delight were invented weeks ahead of time.

The storytellers even enlisted the cooperation of some of the teenagers to dress in costume and play a part. The squaws created colorful costumes and masks for the actors. Those who specialized in dyes were enlisted, and they requested that Powwaw show them where to get the plants, berries, and roots to make the beautiful colors. Special logs were hollowed out for a line of bowls that held multiple wells of color and were set aside in dry areas for the time when the braves and maidens painted their skin.

Everything had to be finished at least a day ahead, as it was necessary to reserve the last day for collecting perishable items such as crabs, oysters, special fish, and mussels. The cool stream running underground began to be crowded with many sunken baskets to keep everything chilled. These baskets were lined with sharkskin to keep the salty seafood from mixing with the fresh water.

This festival was nearing the season of the beaver moon—an excellent time to trap beaver and muskrat. For such an ugly animal, the beaver's fur was the most delicate and softest to be found. The braves had even been trapping rabbit and skunk. The fur of the skunk, with its black and white color, was prized, but it had to be done far ahead of time as the aroma of a disgruntled skunk could stay in the woods for days.

As time went by, certain braves and colonials went again to the mainland and to the midden at Kings Point for more meat—deer especially, and wild boar and hogs if they could find them. They also brought back more shells and a few more pearls. This ongoing process would not stop until the ceremony began. This was also the season for hunting duck of many varieties, Canadian geese, and snow geese, and only the most skilled arrows were sent on this errand.

Ellie was a great help with the younger kids. She kept them occupied, and along with the Indian children they invented many games. Ellie taught them all ring around the roses, which became their favorite game. They had to squat when she called it out, sending giggle fits throughout the camp, putting those in earshot in an even more cheerful mood and lightening their own chores. She was often seen with little Virginia in a sling around her back. Keeping the younger children occupied freed up the women to complete their tasks. Ellie even saw to it that the children were fed, making a game of that also.

Ellie and Sooleawa spent hours in the early evenings working on thinking to other people. They both were new at the experience, and they loved the practice. Most of the time it ended in more laughter than conversation—Ellie because she was of that age, and Sooleawa because she was so fidgety with all the attention. Her girlfriends were busy with setting up surprises, and they did not want her around, fearing they would reveal some secret. Tradition held that the bride and groom did not see each other before the celebration, so that left only Ellie for company. This was just fine with Ellie. Sometimes they would wander down to the practice area to watch the games. Sooleawa only wanted to glimpse Keme, but Ellie was anxious to see the progress that Luke and Blake had made.

Keme, Manteo, and Wematin were not to be found. They were training for rougher sports, such as wrestling. Keme and his friends were also learning a special dance that they would do for his bride. But down near the water, the boys were happily taking a break from their practice, and the young Indian boys, the colonial boys, Luke, and Blake were busy skipping shells across the water. This contest was exciting for all, as everyone was counting skips. So far, Blake was ahead. His shell had skipped at least five times. While the girls watched, Blake was dethroned by a colonial kid who was about his age. It seemed that the younger boys, whose wrists were nimble and true, played this game better.

The Croatoan boys were used to Blake and his skill in picking up sports, but one little colonial boy, John, was getting so good that he was beginning to gain much respect from the Indian boys, who so far had not been swift in befriending the strangers. It was the best thing that could have happened. The little braves began to crowd around the newest winner, because in the events to come, he would be on their team. With much chattering, it appeared that the braves and the colony boys would be entering this competition in the festival. It would serve as a new game, because it did require a bit of skill, and especially since they thought they might have a winner. If the other tribes did not know the game, too bad. This festival was theirs, and John, the colonial boy, was going to win.

Meanwhile, in the village, the wedding arbor was being built out of young sapling trees and vines to make the arch. It was covered in ferns, with shells and feathers woven throughout for color. Also, the dress was finished, and the maidens excitedly asked Weroansqua to come take a look for her approval. She was amazed at the skill of her young girls and the knowledge they had gained from the colonial women. Her eyes shone bright with the beginnings of tears. It was beautiful. She was also shown her dress for approval, but she was so overwhelmed with the bridal dress that she hardly paid any attention to her own.

On display also was a six-foot strap of wampum depicting the tribe's history. Wampum was valued as treasure by Indian tribes as far away as the mountains. Settlers and tribes used it for money. Wampum was made from two special shells. The large quahog clam shell—bigger than most and thicker than all—was of two colors. Most of the shell, from the hinge through the inside, was white, but around the outer edges the color abruptly changed to deep purple. Sometimes even more unique quahog had a graduating lavender color that blended into the heavy purple, and these shells were more valuable. The shells were broken and shaped into small pieces that were washed with sand and water until they were smooth. The clamshell was so thick that a hole could be bored into the middle to allow the shell to be threaded on a thin strip of deer hide and thus be displayed in a pattern or picture. In that way, the white, purple, and lilac pieces were placed in an arrangement designed to portray a story.

The second shell was a whelk, sometimes called a conch. The white parts of this shell, close to the spiral of the whelk, were cut to allow it also to be placed on a string of sorts, adding to the intricacy of the composition. Many of the cut mollusks resembled the shape of macaroni, a tubular rather than round figure.

Wampum represented timeless work, a rare find, and therefore was more special than more readily available varieties. Wampum was sometimes traded to inland tribes for lavish furs from hides of animals not found on the coast. Bear fur was a prized item because of its size and uses, as was beaver for its softness. The coastal areas had a few black bears, but the mountains had many, so both parties valued the trade.

The day of the festival arrived, as did the guests. They came by canoe: large ones for carrying poles for teepees, plus an abundance of supplies, and small ones carrying families. The woods became alive with people, all bringing something for their hosts. The banks had such a long stretch of canoes that no one worried about a surprise attack from across the sound. Surely anyone could see the numbers of warriors in this place, and one could not hope to overcome a force of this magnitude.

The tribes met maybe once a year to join in a celebration of friendship, and the wedding of a chief's daughter was the most momentous occasion of all. Among the invited guests of all three tribes, there was much delight and camaraderie as the elders greeted each other. Visitors were shown to the areas where they would stay, and they began to settle in for the four-day feast of games, renewed friendship, music, and stories that led up to the ceremony. The Indian maidens of the tribes sized each other up, seeing how some had grown beautiful and others not so much. The girls stood around in groups, whispering to each other, not being as forward as the boys. The boys wanted to see if their friends from other villages had grown or gotten stronger. They did not care about beauty as did the girls. Theirs was a survey of the physique. They each looked suspiciously at others they thought would be in their competition, wondering if they would be able to best their opponents once the games began.

The children had not gotten to the point of judgment in their lives, and theirs was the most friendly greeting as they immediately began to play.

The Kinnakeet and Hatorask displayed a little surprise at seeing so many English in the group. However, they had heard, as news travels, that the settlers had been rescued and therefore treated them with respect, welcome, and a little curiosity. These were the first white-skinned, blue-eyed people some of them had ever seen, and they stared openly. The colonials kept to themselves, not wanting to cause the Croatoan any embarrassment or extra work. They assisted the Croatoan with chores that fell to the host to provide for their invited guests. They had made ample mats, had sleeping quarters in the most unusual places, and provided fire spots for all to use so that they would be comfortable.

Most of the Indian braves of all tribes carried a small pouch of flint chunks at their waist used for striking sparks to make a fire. Fire and water extended life. The visiting tribes arrived with their own furs for warmth—and to show wealth, also, the many items necessary for comfort. This group was growing larger, and everybody was concerned with the well-being of the other. Most visitors also came with small teepees for shelter, which the Croatoan greatly appreciated. The teepees were not so large that they could not be transported, and the poles that formed the skeleton of the structures had been used as travois on which to carry away from the canoes and to the wooded areas the items they would need in order to erect their living quarters.

On the second day, after the guests had settled in and rested, the games began. The first was a foot race, which was Blake's specialty. He was fast, and Wematin was readying him for some of the others whom he knew would give Blake a test. Wematin had spent so much time with Blake that they could read each other's signals at a glance. The first race was one of pure speed, and the running course was straight. Many young boys saw themselves as runners, and it was the easiest to practice for. So many entered that several starts were needed to decide which four were the fastest runners. On each side of the track, the Indians and colonials stood three deep, the families of the runners on the first line and supporters behind.

Wematin and Manteo were prominent in their appearance, and probably the most vocal of the crowd. The race was overseen by members of all tribes to prevent questions at the end. Blake was ready, and his face showed determination and focus. He kept his eyes fixed on Wematin and was totally unaware of anyone else in attendance. Wematin placed himself at the finish line, in Blake's direct line of sight. The coach was more nervous than the athlete, who actually was not nervous at all. Before the games, Blake had asked Luke if he was nervous to compete against a brave from Kinnakeet, whom everyone expected to win in his attempts as an expert marksman with the bow. Luke calmly answered that he was never nervous because he had prepared and was ready. Actually, Luke and another Croatoan boy had practiced every night and shared skills, so he was not worried about Kinnakeet. He thought even his friend might be able to best that boy, so as a team, Luke and Smiling Wolf were good competition for the match against another tribe. They had advanced in skill over the last few days.

Blake changed his attitude from that of "I might" to that of "I will," and he grinned a winner's grin when he looked down the line at Wematin. The conch horn blew, and the first race was on. Blake shot out front in the beginning and never slowed down. His feet were flying, and as he neared the end, one of the Hatorask braves began breathing down his back as he approached. Blake simply shifted to a faster gear and shot out ahead, winning the first heat. Wematin almost killed him when he grabbed him to pick him up. Being out of breath, it was almost impossible for Blake to gain a gasp of air as his biggest supporter put him in a tight hug. Finally he was let go, and none too soon. As he struggled for air, everyone thought that it was because he had expended too much energy on the run, but it was because Wematin hugged the breath out of him.

There were several heats after that, and Blake had a chance to size up his opponents. Inside his heart he knew he could beat them, and he told Wematin so. Finally, after a rest period for all runners, the race for the winner was on the line. There were five boys—one of the races had ended in a tie, and both advanced to the finals—all around Blake's age, some a little older. They looked like horses pawing the ground and getting ready to run. Blake just stood calmly in a ready position and stared pointedly at Wematin at the end of the line.

The signal sounded, and they were off. To be truthful, Blake had built up his courage so much that it was never a contest. He took off more leisurely than before and hit his stride about halfway to the finish line. His initial hesitation had fooled the other boys, and they were overly confident, so as he passed them, one by one, they were not prepared and very surprised at being overtaken. Blake flew across the marked line and into the arms of Wematin so hard he knocked him to the ground, and they both lay there rolling around in laughter. The Indian lad was going to miss this boy. He loved him more than he could say, and the feeling was mutual.

Next was the age group for Luke, who also was no slouch as a runner. But his skills did not match the speed of a young brave from the Hatorask, and Luke's second-place finish was a little disappointing. Manteo was still proud of him and showed it, because he also had knowledge that for three different contests—whip accuracy, bow and arrow, and hatchet throwing—not a boy on the island his age could touch him. Luke swallowed his letdown and concentrated on the events to come. Probably losing the first contest was good for him, because his determination was set, and he was ready to go. The other events were not speed but accuracy, and in this Luke had talent.

In knife throwing, Blake's aim was as true as his heart, and the mark placed on the tree was a square center shot for him. One other boy matched him, so there had to be a more complicated trial in order to decide the winner. The mark on the tree was changed to a smaller target, and the boys moved back a couple of feet. Calling Bird, the boy from Kinnakeet, tried first. His knife hit the edge of the target—not outside, but on the rim. Technically he had touched the mark. The crowd from Kinnakeet cheered loudly and hugged each other with confidence. It was expected that they would take home the special carving for this event. Blake set his feet, but after a glance at Wematin he studied his stance and changed his own position to mimic Wematin. His face showed a look of purpose, and he took his time, rolling the knife around in his hand to get the desired grip. This was far away, and he was a little guy, but his determination rose as he drew back and fired the missile so hard it drove the mark dead center, knocking the other knife to the ground. Manteo and Luke got to him first, and Luke and Blake were in such a hug that Manteo had to pick them both up in order to participate in the embrace. The tall Indian threw his head back and laughed at the sky!

Other games commenced. The little colonial boy beat everybody from all tribes at skipping shells and exhibited the biggest grin imaginable. All the boys of the Croatoan gathered around him and hoisted him to their shoulders. It was a glorious spectacle. There was a round of young boys wrestling, and Luke and Blake cheered so hard they had to find water to soothe their throats.

Blake entered the hatchet-throwing event for his age, knowing he wasn't any good, but it was so much fun to compete that he didn't care. He did not even place in the top five. His hatchet landed on the blunt side and fell to the ground, much to the laughter of his friends. His silly grin at the end was testimony that trying was better than watching, and he was satisfied.

"I could knock out the animal, but probably not kill it," he giggled to Wematin, who hugged him anyway. He was also proud of the effort.

By the crowd it drew, the relay race proved to be the most anticipated of all. Because four boys competed on a team, spectators from several families and all of their friends made up the viewing crowd. The boys ran a certain distance, passed a stick to the next teammate, and the first boy of the four to come back to the starting point ahead of the others won. It was a competition of the four best from all the tribes. After Blake's spectacular first race, the boy who was supposed to lead off willingly gave up his place on the relay team to Blake, knowing that he had just lost to him in an earlier race. More than anything, the Croatoan wanted the tribe to bring home the trophy. Blake, first off the block, shot out so fast that none of the other kids could even come close. After he handed off the stick, the second and third boys lengthened the lead. When the stick was handed to the last Croatoan, he dropped it and had to turn abound to pick it up, which took so much time that the other tribes had a better shot at winning, as they had a smaller lead to make up. The last young Croatoan expended all of his energy and, with a lunge at the end, managed to barely reach the finish line first. Barely was enough, and it was over.

Up to this point, the relay was the event of the day. Blake was so excited to win with the other boys that it became the favorite of all the things he did that day.

Luke was up next: bow and arrow. He competed for half an hour trying to best his friend from the Croatoan. As he had thought, they both were better than anyone in the other tribes, and it came down to the two of them. He and his friend Smiling Wolf just refused to lose. Luke hit the target on the tree, dead center. Smiling Wolf shot and split Luke's arrow. Luke shot and split Smiling Wolf's arrow. The game went on until their fingers were raw and their arms tired, and not much arrow was left to split. Finally it was called a draw. The tribes had never seen such a display of marksmanship. It would be spoken of for years to come. Both boys locked arms and walked proudly away in a bit of a swagger around the camp. Two champions were better than one.

Finally came the hatchet throw for Luke's age. This event was also much anticipated. Luke did great, but his hands were so tired and his fingers so raw from his effort with the bow that participating was actually painful for him. In the end, a very skillful and uninjured young brave from Kinnakeet took the victory.

After a break for food, the next to last of the matches for young boys was skill with a whip, which turned out to be the most entertaining of all. As Luke bested one after another, Taregan from Hatorask also won against his opponents, and the game of skill came down to those two. Manteo for the first time felt a little nervous. Taregan was the son of the Hatorask chief, and this contest represented more than one young man against another. First of all, the two older men had each braided the whips. It was Manteo's skill at tightly plaiting multiple strips of hide against Chogan's ability to make a tight weave. If any air came between the braids, the whip would not be as crisp. Each man eyed the other, and their fake smiles told the tale. Luke knew what was at stake, and he was not about to let his mentor down. Taregan, on the other hand, was older and not really concerned with losing to the light-skinned boy who was not as tall nor as muscular as he was. Taregan was named after the crane, and he figured his height would be enough to defeat the shipwrecked stranger from the Croatoan.

The object was to flick a small piece of wood off the stump on which it sat. Both boys, no problem. Second chip, both boys, no problem. They had to make it more difficult. This time, a volunteer threw an object in the air that had to be diverted by the whip before it hit the ground. Both boys also easily accomplished this feat. To everyone's surprise Blake strode into the arena and stood stationary with a small twig sticking out from his mouth. He motioned with his hand for Luke to strike. *Pop!* The twig snapped in half to the ground, while, to everyone's astonishment, the other half was still in Blake's mouth. The crowd gasped in amazement! Luke stepped back, smiling, Blake walked to stand beside him.

"It's a trick!" Taregan shouted. "They cheat!" he snarled loudly enough for Wematin to hear. Wematin stepped forward and challenged Taregan to find a twig. He did so, and it was a little longer than the one Blake had. There was a protest from the watchers as the twig was too long and therefore not an even match. One other Hatorask brave stepped forward to help. He held the twig in his outstretched hand and closed his eyes. Taregan's whip breezed by the outside tip, missing entirely. "It is a trick!" said Taregan again.

Another man stepped forward, from Kinnakeet. "I will find a stick," he said, "and I will hold it in my mouth. Let the Croatoan try again. I am Kinnakeet, and I do not cheat."

Luke took his whip, cracked it a couple of times, and measured the distance, the wind, and his wrist. *Pop!* He again snapped the twig in half without touching the bearer's nose. There was no measure to relay the wildness of the audience. They could not believe their eyes.

Luke motioned to Taregan to try again. There was one problem: there were no takers to hold the stick, so they had to wedge it in the same manner between two logs, with a long piece sticking out. Taregan tried three times to even touch the twig, but it did not happen. He bowed to his opponent in a sportsmanlike fashion and graciously walked away. Chogan was disappointed in the outcome but proud of the way his son had handled himself.

He will make a good chief, he thought, following his son, putting his arm around him, and accepting the defeat, which really had demonstrated the boy's strength.

Other games and events took up most of the afternoon, and finally it was time for the water contests. Swimming was also a crowd favorite, confirmed by the numbers who got in their canoes to row out for a firsthand view. Canoes took the swimmers to the start, and floating logs had been placed earlier to mark the finish line. This was Luke's second specialty, and one that was natural to him. He had a thin, tall, slightly muscular body to crawl across the water, with even, long strokes that hardly made a ripple and such strength in his legs that his kick propelled him forward. In this event he was matched against older boys, but Manteo insisted to the tribe that he could do it. They had been practicing every afternoon. They had also been late for dinner each evening, to Weroansqua's wrath, so she was also in a canoe to see if the time had been worth it.

Luke slipped over the side and waited for the conch to sound. At the first blow he kicked off and never even looked around to see who was chasing him. Actually no one was chasing him. He had it all to himself. He was so light and so fast and so far ahead that Manteo had all he could do to row swiftly enough to the finish line to pick him up. Luke beat the canoe by several minutes and calmly treaded water waiting for his ride back. Manteo was so thrilled that he jumped over the side, clasped Luke tightly, and let the canoe drift away. They ended up both having to swim for that ride. What a scream of noise rose from the watchers as they observed the great Indian swimming after the canoe.

At the end of the day, the prizes were handed out to the winning children, and the company of revelers broke apart and headed toward the blankets of food. Blake and Luke gave their prizes to the colonial young-sters, whose faces made the whole company happy, as they had already been through so much. There were dances and tribal discussions of the day. The events had gone late and light was fading, so the storytellers decided to put off the contests in that area until the children were fresh enough to stay awake. Much had been planned for the storytelling, and they did not want it all to go for naught. The first day had been a success, with all tribes winning enough trophies to make them happy.

The next day was the most exciting, pitting the men against each other in various areas. The most eagerly awaited was the wrestling competition between the braves. While watching the children was fun and had put everyone in a good mood, this event was what every person had come to see. Wrestling was expected to spill over into a two-day affair, as some matches were more physical than others. The participants also needed a rest period between types of tournaments.

Wrestling took place in several arenas, with more than one pairing going on at the same time. The rounds were set up according to size and weight, not age. If there was an older brave who was still strong and powerful, he could be matched against a strapping lad of the same build but years younger. It really was a challenging sport, and each tribe had its favorites. The Croatoan had all their hopes on Wematin, who could best every man in his own tribe. He was not the burliest nor the most muscular, but he was a quick, strapping young man with mental skills unmatched by anyone Manteo had ever seen. He just hoped that Wematin did not get hurt, because these men were serious. It was more than a wrestling match for the tribes. It was a rivalry.

The wrestlers battled all morning and into the early afternoon. Outside the rings there were other contests, but everyone drifted back to one of the circles to watch a favorite or one whom others had hailed as the best. The spectators only drew themselves away from the events to grab a bite of food from the blankets covered with tasty treats and special dishes spread throughout the village. Food was not high on the list of things to do during this part of the games. Match after match, the men grappled—some won, some got hurt, some just lost. By the time it got down to two, it was nearing sunset, and the tribes were jockeying for a position to see the finals.

As Manteo had suspected, Wematin would face Hassun (meaning stone) from the Hatorask tribe. Hassun had won in this arena many times. Sometimes his victories had been disputed, as he was known to cheat. Manteo was determined not to let this happen here, and he was on guard to watch for any illegal or potentially dangerous hold against his brother. The tension in the air permeated all the tribes. Hassun was not a well-liked man, nor was he respected, but he was strong and had proven himself in previous battles in these games, including one where he broke the arm of one of his opponents from his own tribe.

Wematin had stripped down to his loincloth and was lightly oiled, knowing that being heavily oiled would slow him down and cause more physical harm to his skin. Too much oil just allowed the sand to grind into the skin and cause chafes or open sores. Hassun appeared, and he was heavily oiled. He was not concerned about getting himself hurt but rather with hurting his opponent.

The conch blew, and the men squared off. Both circled each other, staring down their foe and looking for an opportunity to strike. The match would be considered won when one brave fell on his back, and Hassun felt this was a no-contest situation since his brawn truly was superior to his younger challenger. Wematin was aware that the heavy older man could beat him, so he was intent on outthinking the huge Indian. Wematin also knew that he had some skills of his own. They circled, and Wematin dove for the feet of the massive brave, hitting him at a side angle. Using his arms, Wematin swept the feet out from under Hassun. The big Indian hit the ground hard, on his butt, and gave off a mighty grunt. But Wematin was also on the ground and had to get away quickly from the long arms of his opponent before he grabbed him and hugged him to near death.

That first blow hurt Hassun. He had been injured when he fell wrong, hitting his hip hard on the sandy ground. As he scrambled to his feet he blindly charged Wematin, and with a quick sidestep Wematin moved out of his way. Now Hassun was angry. He felt he had been made a fool of, and his irritation made him blind to strategy. Time and time again he lunged at the younger brave, only to clasp air. At one point he lunged forward and caught Wematin as he was avoiding the rush and spun him around. Had he hit the chest as he had intended, everything would have been over, as Hassun's weight would flatten the younger and more agile brave. The match continued—ten minutes, then fifteen. Hassun was getting tired, and he was also getting stupid. Wematin was still light on his feet, but knowing that playing keepaway would not win for him, he had to get the older man on his back in order to gain a victory.

Hassun grabbed Wematin around the throat in an attempt to choke him, at the same time making a move that looked like he would poke out an eye. The crowd protested loudly with shouts and loud boos. After all, they had not liked the fact that Hassun had broken a man's arm earlier, so Manteo did not have to worry about cheating. None of the men were going to stand for that. They were looking for skill, and Wematin had been handily defeating his opponent on that mark. Hassun heard the boos and loosened his grip just a little, enough to let Wematin take a breath—and before he could tighten it again, Wematin slipped down from the heavily oiled body, out of the encircling arm of his rival. He hit the ground and scrambled up before the mighty warrior could turn around.

Now they were both on their feet again. Wematin quickly struck before Hassun could gather his thoughts, diving at his feet in the exact same move that had started the match. This time the bigger man hit his rump hard—so hard it stunned him—and Wematin was on him like a cat. He threw his whole body at the big man's upper torso and pinned him to the ground. Hassun's arms splayed out, his head hit hard. He was out! Wematin was so exhausted that he could not even crawl off the massive Indian's head, and Manteo and Loutau lifted him to his feet while the entire male company of Croatoan cheered and then carried Wematin's resting form on their shoulders all around the camp. The Kinnakeet were bringing up the rear, and most of the Hatorask braves were in tow, too. It had been a match to tell stories about.

The big Indian lay still on the ground with very little fanfare around him. He was still there as others walked away. Powwaw strode over and poured sound water on his head, which brought him awake sputtering. Hassun went home before any of the other ceremonies began.

Again the feast that night went late, with everyone enjoying the entertainment while they ate. First came the maiden dance, then the dance of the elders, followed by several typical tribal stomps. These were so lively that the audience joined in, and soon everyone was dancing to the beat of the new sharkskin drums, with ornate and highly polished rattles also keeping the rhythm, and the beautiful lilting sounds of the gleaming and intricately honed whalebone flutes.

The children were fresh from listening to the wonderful tales spun by the storytellers and wanted to follow the actors around. Tonight they were fascinated by the elaborate masks that the dancers wore. Some were scary, as when they did the dance of the snake. Some were comical, as when they danced the dance of the chase, which depicted a young brave chasing down a young maiden for a kiss. They were full of good food, and the elders were full of strong drink. Powwaw had gotten together with the other shaman, and they had created a drink from grapes that had been allowed to ferment. The entire group of merrymakers were happy, full, and mostly tired. It had been a wonderful day, and the next day was more rounds of skilled competitions.   The tribes awakened early, with much to do. There was a rowing contest. The Croatoan had anchored three floating logs out in the sound, and the canoes were manned with each tribe's best. As the drumbeat of the coxswain started at the back of the canoe, the braves pulled their hardest on the paddles to round the log and make it back to the shore first. The crowd was jumping up and down, actually drowning out the drums as they cheered for their favorites. The Kinnakeet took home a magnificent prize.

There were foot races with the men and spear throwing for distance. The maidens of all three tribes did their creative dances, attended by all the young braves of the tribes. Storytelling continued, and the children moved from story to story in rotation.

The grown men had their skill tested with bow and arrow. Wematin beat Manteo in the last and final match. At that time every man was

Croatoan, and it was the old against the young. Blake hugged Wematin's knees until he thought his teacher would topple to the earth. Manteo was as proud as if he had won, and he had tried. He had no intention of allowing his little brother to win. The women had their fry bread contest, and it turned out to be a draw. Not one person could attest to which was the best. Even the braves knew when to shut up. The men walked around carrying large smoked turkey legs, as every tribe provided almost a small canoe full of them. It was the season, and each wanted in a way to prove which tribe was the best at providing.

After the evening meal, everyone participated in another show of tribal dances and silly skits—each more elaborate and expressive than the other. They told stories with their footwork and hand gestures, and their costumes showed the beadwork and skill that had gone into the beauty of them all. The games lasted all day, the feast was great, and companies were tired. Tomorrow was the wedding. Sleep seemed like a good idea.

★ 13 ★

The Wedding

The morning began with an onslaught of small yellow butterflies. They came off the sound into the camp and through the woods for half the morning. They usually arrived once or maybe twice a year. Always in a rush, always so many, and they were everywhere. Other times of the year the monarch and many other colorful butterflies visited the island, but these hundreds of little yellow droplets of sun were the most welcomed festive treat—and here, on the day of the wedding.

The camp was abuzz. Everyone was up, moving around. The young maidens were either bathing or, having chosen to do so predawn, were now applying paint and creating intricate hair designs. The delightful colors of bird feathers were on display in rows of trays side by side. In another area, the same could be said for pots of beautiful paint, accompanied by recognized and talented Indian artists, including those from the neighboring tribes on hand to create a theme imagined by a brave, maiden, or chief.

Also in the middle of the compound, the arch was getting its finishing touches. The sides were covered in vines, intertwined with white honeysuckle, grown wild and transplanted. There was a fur platform, and tall, stripped-bare straight pines made the poles of the arch. Limbs of the mimosa tree in bloom overlapped and enclosed the top. The ceremonial poles were billowing with long stretches of vine and bleached hide covered with beads, shells, and feathers. The center pole was wrapped with white deer-hide strips entwined from bottom to top, with four-foot streamers floating in the breeze. The air was crisp and clean—a wonderful fall day, with all the smells of a feast. The blankets surrounding the encampment were already crowded with wooden trays, sanded and polished, full of homemade treats. There was a wooden bowl with disks of cornbread and bowls of fruit. In another area was a kettle of corn mash for dipping. It was a communal gathering, and all were getting ready for one huge ceremony, followed by the happy celebration.

Dancers were in lodges applying makeup, and chanters were putting on the face of the characters they would play. All tribes displayed skill and beauty on this day. Their hosts had been generous, and today it was all about honoring the host tribe and its celebration.

Weroansqua was already in full ceremonial trappings—not wedding attire, but formal robes. She had on the long, flowing deer-hide cape of command. The cloak was gray. The entire skin had been blasted with a blue-dyed wash and bleached to a soft blue-gray. When the light was right, it was silver. Her leggings were the same, as were her boots. She moved to the back of the lodge to sneak out to the cave portion and the room where Sooleawa was getting dressed. There was much commotion and laughter coming from the end of the cavern. Lit with torches and shafts of daylight, Weroansqua watched as Sooleawa tried on her wedding dress.

Powwaw had been up since the rim of the sun was still below the horizon. As the sun rose, so did the ritual he performed. His fire was high and had a blue center cast. His powder was potent as he blessed the sun for this day. The blue cloud floated toward the trees, disappearing in a wisp of a wolf's head. He smothered it and lifted the blanket to send up another wisp, this time a raven. He smothered it again, this time revealing a twist of smoke in the form of the whelk, and away it went.

Manteo, Wematin, and Loutau all had long robes of leadership laid out for them. The deerskin pants had been beaded and sewn with shafts of feathers falling down the outside leg. Manteo had a wide wampum belt showing his power in the tribe. It was braided on thin white strips of hide that frayed at the ends. His cape, colored the under-feather of teal, draped across his shoulders and reached the ground. The ornamentation around the bottom was crow's feather, almost blue-black. Manteo had in his hand a headband of deer hide beaded with tiny wampum shells. He stood at the entrance of his wigwam, leaning on the log support shaped from a mature tree, and looked at the ceremonial poles. Manteo had never seen them white. With their masks showing it emphasized the figures dramatically: Kitcki, the Great Spirit, the raven; the wolf; death; Mooin, the bear, with paw prints leading to the top where the bear head was. The mask of war was on one pole, carved from bottom to top, and another pole offered a she-wolf with cubs in a tree hollow.

Blake visited Mingan for the last time at the carver's request. Ellie was watching every move that Sooleawa made, like a shadow and just as quiet. Luke was helping Wematin polish a huge turtle shell he intended to give to the bride and groom. The shell was almost three feet around, a beautiful snapping turtle shell all greens and brown. Wematin had it polished to a high-shine finish. This was an unusual type of turtle: an alligator snapper, with a horned shell that looked like the scales of an alligator. Bigger than most, it was impossible to catch, but once Wematin saw it, he had to have it for his sister. He knew the danger of going after such a prize, but they were hunting near Alligator River across on the mainland, and it was crawling through the marsh to the river. Wematin grabbed it, lifted it up, and threw it sideways to rest at the feet of the other braves. They scattered, and he laughed—careful not to get near the dangerous jaws—rolled it on its back, and stabbed it in the throat.

The jaws could have broken his arm, but he handled the snapper with skill and therefore was not injured. A snapper never lets go, so they are usually left alone. This gift was special, and befitting a great celebration the squaws made a stew from the meat.

Throughout the village, people were stirring, shaking off the events of the days before and preparing for the wedding. Everyone had a task and was busy at it. The air buzzed with excitement. Powwaw and other shamans were deep in conference, looking for signs of the future of the chosen two. Powwaw's ceremonial fire was now joined by two others, and they read the signs. It was not lost on Sucki that he had been left out of the group of shaman, and he resented the exclusion. This disrespect only fueled his anger at not being given enough credit for the successful rescue. He was always walking in Powwaw's shadow, and he felt that he also was gifted with special powers—no matter that they were dark powers.

He went to his cave and lit a fire of his own. In Sucki's fire there was a snake with bright red eyes. As it rose from the fire it dripped venom from its fangs. Sucki prayed to the snake, and with his eyes closed he gave a final hand motion over the flames. The snake disappeared.

Powwaw was aware of the fire of the conjuror, knowing that eventually they would have to clash. He did not look forward to the confrontation, but he would be prepared.

The company began to gather in the ceremonial area. There were blankets laid out covered with food and another huge basket full of smoked turkey legs—also pots of squash and corn mash, fruits and melons. Fish was frying on the outskirts of the village, as was a pot of venison. Hollowed-out logs served as casks for drinks and were scattered about, with gourds attached for dipping out the contents.

The dancers began to come to the area where they would perform, and within minutes the first blast from the huge whelk was sounded. The area began to fill up with the most elaborately dressed moving to the front, near the area designated for the chiefs. Mats and fur platforms were placed in specific areas close to the arbor. The second flourish from the conch sounded, and Weroansqua appeared with her hand on the arm of Loutau, her brother, followed by Manteo and Wematin. They were a magnificent sight. All were wearing deer-hide capes that reached the ground. Manteo, Wematin, and Loutau had designs painted down their arms and across their chests. Loutau had on a long headdress reaching his waist, with cascading feathers from crown to sides. He looked every bit the brother of a chief. Manteo had two tall, blue heron feathers attached to a hide headdress that was solidly beaded and tied at the back of his ebony hair. He wore a four-strand necklace of bones separated by the teeth of shark and colored beads. His boots were of soft diamondback rattlesnake skins, almost reaching his knee. Manteo's pants were bleached deer hide, matching the color of his cape. He cut a striking figure.

Wematin had a cape of deer hide colored to a blue tint that was slung over one shoulder. His hair was also tied back with one braid down the back. His headband was a string of braided hide holding the red feathers of the red-winged blackbird. Wematin's boots were sharkskin, their silver color enhanced by the blue cast of the hide cape. Across his bare chest was a vest of porcupine quills that were placed together in a design that covered four rows across the front of his body. On Wematin's wrists were cuffs of deer hide dyed to match his cape. He carried the massive turtle shell and placed it at the edge of the raised arbor. The turtle was a sign of the earth and longevity, indicated especially by the size of the shell.

Weroansqua was seated on a special stump that had been carved around the sides with designs of the wolf. The white wolf appeared out of the forest and lay down beside the queen. Visitors also noticed a huge black raven fly to a tall pine, and his dark eyes surveyed the entire area. The chief was dressed magnificently in a tunic made from several hides that had been bleached and recolored to a purple hue. It was made to hang from her shoulders to her boots, with sleeves that reached the elbow. The hides had been chewed to the softness of silk and were free of any adornment. It floated as Weroansqua walked.

But her necklace truly caused a stir among the tribes. It was made of white rabbit fur—the bottom sitting on her collarbone and the top under her chin. There were long staves of soft whale cartilage attached from the bottom row to the top, giving shape to the wide choker, which was adorned with pearls and abalone shells that picked up the sunlight and cast multiple colors on the arbor floor. Her headpiece was the most striking of all, sitting on her head like a crown. It was made of whale staves for height and stiffness, accented with white feathers and swan down. Woven throughout the feathers were the pieces of cut round mirror winking from underneath the wispy feathers, and in the middle was the most magnificent irregular pearl. At the peak of the crown and around the bottom was albino rabbit fur. How could a bride outshine this chief?

As the couple moved toward the arbor, accompanied by Powwaw, Sooleawa was struck by the beauty of it all. Keme had approached her at the edge of the village and took her hands in his. He looked every bit a warrior. He wore as a necklace the claws of the bear he had killed, adding to the magnificent white cape he wore, which was appropriate for a groom. His shroud was made from several hides sewn together to reach the ground. But unlike others in the wedding party, his shroud was double the size. He would end the ceremony by wrapping his bride in the mighty cape to signify the oneness of the pair.

Sooleawa was dressed in multiple deer hides bleached white. The fringe of the first skin dropped from the yoke at the neck, around the arms, and across the chest and back. At the V of the neck was beaded the beautiful head of a wolf. His golden eyes were kind, and the tips of his fur glistened with crushed pearl. At her waist was a wide deerskin belt dyed blue and shaped in a diamond to add width. At the thick part of the belt was the design of the rising sun, made from Atlantic yellow cowrie shells, radiating out from the middle with rays of the smallest, most delicate pearls pointing outward from the yellow beaded sun. This was a sign of good health throughout the body. The hem of the garment was frayed with fringe anchored by tiny pearls. The edge of the hem was uneven, touching the ground on two sides, and was short to show the boot in other sections. Sooleawa's boots were made of sharkskin and edged with tiny pearls. Her hair was loose and flowing. She had tufts of snow geese feathers centered with pearls in her hair and carried a white wild rose.

The ceremony began as a soft drumbeat, along with Powwaw chanting his charms and weaving the smoke from a pipe. The village was softly quiet, with only the aroma of the burning incense of Powwaw's good-luck wishes and the soft, muffled sound of the sharkskin drum. The small clubs used to strike the drum were covered in beaver fur, intended not to disturb the silence. The couple held hands with the old shaman, and Weroansqua placed her hand on the white wolf, each wishing good fortune for the two.

Powwaw's face turned ashen as he glanced at the bowed heads of the masses of people and saw a snake slithering its way down the middle of the crowd and toward the front. The others were so caught up in the moment that they did not see the intruder. Powwaw lifted his head toward the peak of the smoke circling overhead and sent an urgent thought to the wolf. The wolf was already beyond the thought. It was muscled up and ready to strike the minute the snake slithered in front of him.

The snake had been delivered to the ceremony in an elaborately covered basket, placed among the pile of gifts located at the ceremony's entrance. The wolf, however, smelled the snake the moment it came within the compound area and followed the scent of evil until the particular basket had been placed at the entrance to the arbor. The wolf—head down, eyes cast upward and gleaming—watched the basket intently until he saw it move. His golden eyes narrowed. At that moment, Weroansqua winced with knowing and placed her hand on the neck of the wolf at her side, felt the tense muscles, and knew it was ready.

The reptile moved beyond the crowd and, to Powwaw's shock, curled to strike. This time, Weroansqua and Manteo saw the coiled mass, but they were too late. The wolf caught the snake in midair and, with one mighty snap of his head, severed the snake in half, at which time it disappeared in a wisp of smoke. The quick motion of the wolf caught the stunned crowd by surprise, and they looked around, wondering what had just happened. Left on the ground near the foot of the altar was the rattle of a huge timber rattlesnake—eight rattles, each over an inch long. Powwaw picked it up and put it in his tunic pouch, thinking that it would make an excellent charm for future use. Sooleawa and Keme had not seen the spectacle, as their backs were turned and heads bowed. Only three people were privileged to the sight, and those three were sure they knew the culprit.

At the end of the ceremony Keme wrapped his large cape around his bride. Then Sooleawa and Keme left the gathering and followed a procession of Indians dressed in loincloth, with black masks painted across their eyes, into the woods where a feast had been set in their honor. They were seated on the bear rug fashioned from the animal Keme had slain, and under which they would eventually sleep. They were in a special clearing away from the revelers, served by maidens whose eyes were painted into black masks and dressed in white simple tunics. A portion of the meal was the special turtle soup, courtesy of Wematin. It was finally their time alone.

The company began to move toward the ceremonial posts, taking seats on the mats provided in order to enjoy the dances and rituals that would be on display. The dances were intricate, with masks the children loved. One mask was made entirely of an alligator head. Another was the head of the bear, with ears attached and the fur cascading down the sides of the head. Yet another mask depicted an eagle with a long, hooked beak. Each did a dance to the music of flutes carved from the hollow whalebones, with holes for making sound, and the longest bone of the crane, also hollow, to create a different sound. Each flute had a sound unique to its size and length, and the position of its holes. The drums were from all tribes—some tightly stretched deer hide, some sharkskin, and one was a large turtle shell upside down, its underbelly covered in a taut animal hide. All were fastened to their bases with tree resin. Each drum was unique and painted with intricate designs.

Multiple dances took place that afternoon. Each tribe displayed their favorite and wore their most elaborate costumes.

The unmarried maidens were set to begin their dance directed at the unmarried males. Each tribe had created its own version of this dance, as the maidens of all tribes were at a wedding, thinking about a wedding, and looking for a wedding mate. As they danced around the unsuspecting single male guests, they paid special attention to ones they had picked out as a prospect for marriage. The colonials stood at the back but were motioned to move forward by Weroansqua, as she wanted them to see the best of Indian living. This would not happen again, and it was a time of sharing.

When Sooleawa and Keme had finished their private meal, they were accompanied by their servers, and all came back to the gathering to enjoy the dances and music. At a particular time, Keme did his bridal dance for Sooleawa. It depicted a warrior protecting his mate. Several of his friends played the villains to Keme's hero. It was a lively dance, as the drums signaled the danger and also the success of the warrior.

Powwaw's drink was especially enjoyed, and the shamans' concoctions from other villages were plentiful. There was a large pit at one edge of the compound filled with brush and twigs, and resting on top were rocks carried over from the mainland. The fire was stoked white hot and then covered with more rocks. As the rocks heated up, they were covered with oysters, blue crabs, scallops, clams, mussels, and seaweed to steam them open and cook them slightly. The guests filled their wooden bowls with the freshly prepared seafood. There were deerskin sacs hanging from the low branches of trees from which the Indians gathered fresh water brought from the stream. Everywhere were grapes, melons, berries, and corn cakes soaked in honeysuckle.

Powwaw did not discuss with the other shamans the incident with the snake. He did not want them to know of any disfavor among his people. He contacted Weroansqua, and between them they thought out a plan to deal with Sucki, who by now knew his magic was not as strong as the wolf's. No doubt, he was making plans of his own as he began gathering up his lodge. He would have to go away—and soon. He knew the celebration would protect him for a while, but when it was over, they would begin to look for him.

Sucki kept a keen eye on the entrance to the caves. He knew that he had time, as long as the guests were still in the camp. Sucki thought to slip out of one of the rear exits of the cave and into the forest before the ceremonial revelries ended. He had at least twenty-four hours, as it would take that long for the visitors to break down their temporary lodges and say their good-byes. He hurriedly gathered his belongings and packed them in weed baskets. Sucki considered a travois but rejected the thought as the poles would leave a trail, and the talented braves were keen enough to follow a snake. Being the snake he was, he tried to outthink his pursuers.

He needed a fire, but that was impossible until he could be in a place where the smoke would be obscured from the tribe. Sucki also knew that Powwaw's medicine was strong enough to see him in his own fire, so it was necessary for Sucki to be out of the area, with a conjuring fire of his own, and somewhere that Powwaw could not track him. Two shamans warring was an interesting predicament. The good vs. evil contest that faced everyone now faced Sucki. He was convinced that evil would win, not considering Weroansqua's added strength.

It took only a couple of hours for the conjurer to collect his belongings. Throwing the baskets on his back—dressed in a dark cloak that reached the ground and covered his head, with only his eyes showing—he skulked out the back entrance of the cave and into the forest. He was headed to the beach.

Upon arrival, he walked to the left, toward where the island formed a point out into the ocean. Here he tested the direction of the wind. Satisfied that it was blowing away from the camp, Sucki gathered kindling and wood and made his fire as close to the water as possible. Water, a conductor of thought, was his connection to the evil spirits he sought. Whatever evil existed in the ocean, he intended to join up with it, because he had now destroyed his existence on this land.

Because of his dark raiment, one could not discern who this figure was, as he crouched, cloaked and hovering, over a fire and uttered chants. The figures began to show themselves in the smoke. One after another, the monsters of the deep appeared above him: the great white shark; then, swirling and twisting around, the blue-ringed octopus; the frilled shark of the very deep, with his gills spread wide, making his head look like a cobra; and the giant squid. Next came a dark, thick cloud—first a solid mass and finally changing into a form that resembled Sucki himself— that arose into the smoke and disappeared.

The three English children sat around the decorated posts and watched the dances. They had heavy hearts as they felt inside that this was the last time they would see their new—or old, as was the case— family. They sat together, clutched hands, and leaned into each other for comfort. As the ceremonial fire leaped into the air, a blue and silver flame shot out from the middle, and Ellie looked around. She saw Powwaw standing near the edge of the clearing where the trees and paths to the caves were located. He motioned for them to go to him. As the children slipped away from the fire, they stood in front of the old shaman, and he leaned down and kissed each of them in the middle of the forehead. At that he vanished in a puff of smoke, and in his place stood the white wolf. The wolf began to walk slowly down the path into the woods near the caves, and the children followed.

Luke held out his hands, and each child grabbed one, trailing the white wolf. As the forest grew thicker and thicker, the dense, twisted limbs of huge live oaks shielded them from the sky. A slight rain began to fall, and they were back to the clearing where they first met Manteo.

"We need to find our way out of these woods, back to the beach—," Luke started to say, and a thunderclap interrupted his sentence. The flash of light that followed was sharp, and the children closed their eyes against it. When they awoke, they were at the edge of Jennette's sedge, and the small oak trees where they had taken shelter were just ahead. At their feet was a deer hide, and inside it was their English clothes. They reluctantly took off the wedding tunics and put on the clothes they had not seen for a while.

"What will we do with these?" asked Ellie. She didn't want to throw away the beautiful, soft dress she had worn at the wedding. And the boots were the most special Ellie had ever seen, and she so hated to destroy them.

"We will bury them," said Luke. "We will bury them and maybe come back and bring a canvas to keep them in—or a box."

Blake held out his hand to Luke. He was holding something. Luke took the object and flashed the biggest smile. It was a beautifully smooth carved whale, from a bone. Blake's grin was more telling than any words. He had stopped at Mingan's earlier, knowing inside that they would be leaving, and he wanted something he could carry with him. For Ellie, he had chosen a tiny ivory wolf, like the white wolf. And, for himself, even though he had his wolf, he chose a dolphin carved from the whale's bone. They were so small and so comforting to hold. It was like holding on to a spirit.

The carver had hailed Blake one afternoon. During all the visits and deliveries, they had become friends. Blake had shown so much respect for the old Indian. His was a solitary job and one not so much appreciated, but the art he created made people happy. When used as gifts as at the games, his carvings had no equal. But carving was sometimes a lonely job. Blake had helped the old man fill his hours. Mingan chatted with the young boy, who may or may not have understood him, but at least he listened. Not many people want to sit and listen to an old person. He felt passed over until Blake came along, and for a little while he came alive with the life he had lived and was pleased that somebody wanted to hear about it.

He had so appreciated the boy that he beckoned Blake to his cave and showed Blake the items he had carved from the baleen of the whale. He motioned to Blake to choose, and Blake held up three fingers sheepishly. He did not want to ask, but he had to. The other children would never see these. They had only been to the old man's hut one time and were always too busy to go back. Besides, Luke had a friend in Powwaw, and this old gentleman was Blake's special friend, so he was comfortable asking him for a favor. Mingan understood that this was not greed. He had seen the three children and their bond, so he actually had carved the white wolf for Ellie but had not shown it to anyone. He offered. Blake then chose the whale for Luke, because Luke was the mightiest creature in the universe. When Blake hesitated further, the old man handed him the dolphin. "You will be friends," he indicated with his hands to his heart, and he repeated it. So Blake stuck them in the leather pouch the old man had given him and tied it to his waist. This pouch accompanied another on the other side—his flint, for starting a fire. He would never again be without it.

Ellie rolled the wolf around and around in her hand, feeling its smoothness, and also feeling very comfortable and secure. The sprinkle of rain was just starting as the sand showed tiny little droplets here and there.

"Maybe we can get home before the rain starts," said Ellie, and they stood and looked at each other in a bit of a dream state. They felt a little sleepy, kind of tired, and maybe if it had not been about to rain, they all might have dropped under the oaks and taken a nap.

Luke stepped forward. "Let's get going. I'm feeling tired."

"Me, too. I think we've been gone a long time, and Grandmom will be worried," said Blake.

They all took a few stumbles forward, then picked up the pace. Home seemed for some reason to sound pretty good, and this group was adventurous. They walked down by the wash, away from the dunes and soft sand to where it was pressed hard by the receding waves and left dry as the tide went out. They made better time, and Luke picked up a flat shell and skipped it across the calm ocean. At that, the games were on again. Their energy returned, and Ellie became judge to a spirited contest of skipping the shell. They played the game all the way home, their shoes tied and slung over their shoulders, their pants rolled up. Ellie had her leggings pushed up to her knees, and they were wet as far as they could be. She skipped ahead backward so that she could easily count the bounces, and abruptly she stumbled over a log that had washed up behind her as the surf receded and landed on her rump. She was now wet from the waist down, and the happy smile left her face as she realized her predicament. As she wrinkled the corners of her mouth to cry, Luke plopped right down beside her in the surf, and with his hand he splashed water in her face. His grin was so convincing that she forgot her situation, because now it was shared by Luke and Blake, who slid on his knees toward them, pushing the surf in front of him. Now all of them were wet.

When they arrived at the main keeper's quarters, Ellie waved a silent good-bye and scampered into the house and up the stairs to the bedroom facing the front overlooking the lighthouse. She threw off her wet clothes and shoved them in a corner to be dealt with later. Ellie could smell Grandmom's cooking. After brushing off all the sand around her and from the bed, she slipped on another dress and dry leggings, flopped across the bed, head facing the window, and deeply slept with the sound of the familiar, soothing surf in her dream.

The boys repeated the same motion as they went up the stairs to their shared bedroom. By the time Nett checked on them to see where they went, she saw their wet clothes lying in a heap on the floor. Luke had on a dry shirt and pants, and he had stretched out on his bed, bare feet dangling over the side, like he just could not make it all the way. Blake had on one of Luke's shirts that was too big for him, but which he insisted on wearing anyway. They were a little wet as she could see from their hair—not dirty—and totally asleep. So she left the room after shutting the window to keep them from getting a chill from their wet heads.

She thought, *What in the world have they been up to? What did they do this afternoon to get so wet?* as she gathered up the damp clothes and looked at all the sand. She wondered if having two active boys would be the death of her. But Nett was quite happy having boys. They were a challenge, but so loving, and she wanted them to be boys. So what if it meant sweeping the sand out more times than she could count? It was worth it.

The sea air was crisp, and the dolphins used the soft wind to do acrobatics. Their high-pitched squeals penetrated Blake's sleep, and he ran his finger over the carved tooth and fell back asleep. He dreamed of the sea and of the crashing waves that took him to a place where he could play with the dolphin for real. He imagined a ride out to the middle of the ocean on the back of a dolphin who was his friend. Here he met the great turtle, the one who held up the earth, and fled from the mighty shark, only to be saved by a whale.

★14★

Pass the Peas

The children slept so heavily that neither Grandmom nor Nett could awaken any of them for supper. They slept through the night, but just after Christo crowed, Ellie heard a rock hit her window, and she leaned up to see what was going on. Outside, she saw her two companions, dressed and motioning for her to come down. Ellie had slept in her clothes, so it was no problem to silently creep downstairs and meet them. At the front porch they all turned—only to face Grandpop, who had just come down from servicing the light. He began his day at sunrise, when he went back up to the beacon to extinguish the flame.

"What are you three doing up so early in the morning? Didn't you worry your grandmom enough by not taking supper last night? And did you forget this is Sunday, and in a couple of hours we will be getting ready for church? Don't think you are off to play again." Grandpop scowled as he looked down at the guilty faces that stared back.

"Grandpop," said Luke, the spokesman for the culprits, "we were just going to check out the beach to see what washed up last night. We will be right back to get ready for church, and we know we haven't had breakfast, so don't worry. We are all hungry, so we'll be back soon."

The explanation satisfied Grandpop, and it actually was the truth. But the bigger truth was that they wanted to talk about their adventure. Guess that would have to wait. They ran fast down to the beach and plopped down on the sand.

"What do you think? Blake and I have been talking about our adventure, but we wanted to see what you said." Luke was looking intently at Ellie's face.

"I don't know what to think," she said. "I have known for a while that I could hear you both think, but I thought it was because I think *like* you, so I got used to it."

"I can do it, too," said Blake, not wanting to be left out of this older person conversation. "But do you think we will ever go back? I really liked Wematin, and I liked Mingan, and I liked all the things we did, and I want to do it again. Should we talk to Grandmom about it?"

"Not yet," Luke answered. We need to talk it out among ourselves first. We need to go over all the things we saw and heard in the dream Powwaw gave us. There are some things I think I heard, but I want to hear what you both saw and heard. We can't go to Grandmom until we know what to say."

"Well, you heard Grandpop. We need to be careful and not cause any trouble all day long, because I don't want a switching," said Ellie.

"Why would Grandpop switch us? We haven't done anything wrong, I don't think." Luke was not exactly sure how long they had been gone. He needed to know that before he started confessing to things he didn't even know he did.

So they decided that they would hurry back and get ready for church early to make everybody happy, and eat a big breakfast, which would make them even happier. They stood up, brushed off the sand, and of course, raced back to the compound.

When Ellie came back, it was still early, but Grandmom was in the kitchen already. Ellie walked into the kitchen, put her arms around her waist, and gave her a big hug.

"How do you feel this fine morning, my little chickadee?" said Grandmom, crooking out her arm with white hands raised up in the air and catching Ellie close to her in an affectionate squeeze. "You were gone all day yesterday. I missed you. Where did you go?"

Ellie swallowed hard. *Uh-oh*, what was she going to do now? Ellie looked up at Grandmom and said in a little voice, "Grandmom, like you tell me sometimes, it is a long story. Can I tell you later? I'm sorry I wasn't here by supper, but I fell in the surf playing with Luke and Blake, and I got wet, so I came home to change clothes, and I just got sleepy and took a nap. I guess it lasted too long. I want to tell you about it, but I only want to tell *you*."

Odessa wiped her hands on a dish towel and turned toward the little girl. She looked at her face, and she knew. Odessa was no stranger to dreams. She knew what Ellie was going to say. After all, Odessa was the first one to be affected. Inside, she smiled because she knew how strange that first dream felt, and Ellie was only ten—but, by now, a very wise ten-year-old.

"Run along, child. Go put on your pink dress and good shoes. The preacher is coming for dinner after church, and a special ball game is this afternoon, so the compound will be busy. I promised your grandfather I would make a cake for the company, and this afternoon I'm frying up some chicken, so run along. I'll be up there presently and we can talk. Go on now. You still have your breakfast to eat, and we don't want to make your grandpop late for church." Grandmom gave Ellie another squeeze and put her hand on her butt and gave her a little shove. "We can talk later when I come up to do that messy hair. On second thought, that hair is such a mess—draw some water and take it to the back porch. I'm going to wash it before breakfast. Matter of fact, you need a bath!"

Grandmom began to scurry around getting her cake ready, and Ellie went to the back porch where the pump was and began filling the old galvanized tub on the porch. She pulled the sheet across the area to shield the tub. Even she knew she needed a bath.

Next door, it wasn't so easy for Nett.

"Oh, Mommmm," whined Blake, "do I have to?"

"Son, there's no way you are going to church like that! I haven't seen that much sand in somebody's hair since . . . since . . . since never! Now go do what I tell you, and tell Luke, too, and don't even think to make your grandfather late today. Preacher's coming. Now git!"

Blake hurried along to tell Luke the preacher was coming. The preacher's daughter was sweet on Luke, and it would be a great pleasure for Blake to watch Luke squirm all afternoon. Both went out back to the shower their dad had fashioned. Bill was a very talented man when it came to fixing things. He was a machinist's mate in the navy, and handy with plumbing tools also, and he was always tinkering around the assistant's quarters, trying to duplicate some of the modern conveniences he had while growing up in New York. Running water was one of his constant worries. He wanted indoor plumbing, and he wanted electric lights. But so far, the island was not ready for that, and they would have to do with outhouses, kerosene lamps, and hand pumps from the cistern.

The children were ready, clean, shined, and sitting like three innocents on the swing when Grandpop flew out the front door in his quick walk, and in his civvies—a regular suit and tie—looking stern and purposeful. Ellie shoved his Sunday-go-to-meeting hat at him.

"Okay, men, time to go . . . Ellie, go get your grandmother and tell her I'm going to leave her if she doesn't get out here. Luke, where's Nett? She late, too?" he bellowed. You didn't want to mess with Pop when he was in a hurry. It was Ellie's job to hand him his hat when he was hurrying to get out the door, and this day she did not forget.

Charlie Gray was a community man. He was, of course, head of the Lightkeeping Service, but he also was superintendent of the Sunday school, and teacher of the men's Bible class, and he served on the Board of County Commissioners for the island. And those days where he was on business other than the lighthouse, he was dressed in a suit and a fedora. Every so often he had to make the trip to Manteo, the county seat, and project plans for the island. But today he was primed and ready for church and the preacher coming to dinner, plus getting everybody out of the house.

Bill always stayed behind to take care of all the other duties. He did not go to church with the others. William Peter Finnegan was a Catholic from New York who met and married Jeanette when the navy first sent him to assist with the Cape Hatteras Light. And unfortunately for Bill, there was no Catholic church on the island. So Sundays were a day off for Captain Charlie, and he became a civilian for one day a week. It was like a rest for him. He loved doing all that he did. He was born and raised on the island. His father was stationed with the Coast Guard at the Little Kinnakeet Station during Charlie's childhood, and when he was old enough he was sent to a military boarding school on the mainland, because at that time, in Kinnakeet, there was only a one-room schoolhouse that half the time didn't have a teacher—just a volunteer from the village. Grandpa—Amblick Thomas Gray—was determined that Charlie would be well educated.

Nett came walking down the walkway, Grandmom appeared on the porch, and Grandpop brought around the car. The kids piled in the back, the adults in the front. Only a few times did Grandpop have to turn around to calm them down. They all liked going to Sunday school and church. Well, for the three youngsters, Sunday school was great. It was church they had to endure.

They arrived at the white clapboard wooden church in the center of Buxton just in time to see Mr. Nash pulling the long rope that rang the big iron bell in the steeple. It was a great sound, heard all over the village—a call to worship. The bell's clang did not reach all the way out to the lighthouse, so its melodious tone was just majestic when the children got to listen. The bell was one of the best things about church.

The men were usually standing around in the yard talking, and the women were inside, going over recipes or sharing gardening tips.

Everybody hurried inside to find their seats. Charlie Gray began the prayer to start the morning, and then Miss Myrtle got to the piano, and it was hymn time. Miss Myrtle always played the piano—not very well, a few sour notes here and there, but nobody was about to tell her, because nobody else wanted the job. They usually sang a few songs, and then everybody went to their classrooms for Bible study. Funny thing about Miss Myrtle: she had black gums. And when she smiled, you could see those white teeth and black gums, and it was funny. Miss Myrtle made the best pone bread on the island. Everybody said so. But pone bread was made with molasses, and Ellie's theory was that her gums were black from eating too much pone bread. When Grandmom made it, everybody in the family thought it was a treat, but Ellie never touched it. She was determined not to have black gums. No matter that nobody else had the affliction. Ellie was taking no chances.

Grandpop stood in front of the church with hymnal in hand and led the singing. This was a special part of the ceremony, watching everybody sing. Miss Myrtle was loud, competing with the piano as she sang, and watching Pop was funny as he would sing and go up on his tiptoes when the note was high. Luke was singing and going up on his tiptoes for the high notes, and Grandmom popped him on the head. Of course, that delighted Blake, who got the snickers, and Ellie had to pop him. All over the church there was some head slapping going on.

Finally it was time to go to the back of the church where the Sunday school classes were held. The boys were all speed walking—walking so fast it was just below a run—to claim the seats by the window. There they could play with the wasps and dirt dobbers and look out the window, while the girls sat prissily in their dresses, ruffled socks, and Mary Jane shoes. Miss Arnetta was the teacher. Every once in a while she would ask somebody a question, so it was important to divide your attention between what the boys were doing and what Miss Arnetta said. That way, you could pretend to listen and not have your parents get involved.

Parental discipline was the most dreaded threat the children could hear. It always worked. If you got in trouble somewhere, you would always get a double dose of punishment when you got home. If it were up to the kids on the island, every poplar tree would be cut to the ground. It was the preferred tree for cutting switches. The other thing they could do without was the hairbrush—for several reasons.

Miss Arnetta was going on about learning Bible verses, and the boys were swatting wasps. The window was open, and this particular one had no screen. Georgie Tolsen was busy in the back of the room, stirring up mischief so that Allison Quidley would notice, when he saw a huge butterfly on a hydrangea bush outside the window. He quietly slipped his chair back as far as he could and over next to the window. When Miss Arnetta turned her back to the other side to hear a recitation of verses from Macy Farrow, Georgie reached out as far as he could to capture the butterfly. Just as he was off kilter, halfway out the window with his butt out of the chair, Miss Arnetta saw him and said in a loud voice, "Georgie Tolsen!" Poor Georgie thought she had called on him to recite, and here he was half out the window and unstable on his chair. He sort of stood, lost his balance, and as he was going out the window into that hydrangea bush he shouted out,

"Jeeeesusssss weeept," and over the ledge he went. "Jesus wept" happens to be the shortest verse in the Bible, and when Georgie heard that, he knew he had Miss Arnetta cold should she decide to call on him, and he knew she would. He had been saving that verse since the assignment began a couple of Sundays ago, but he lost his mind over Allison Quidley and that butterfly, ruining his chances to be considered studious.

Allison Quidley was the first to giggle, and then everybody rushed to the window to see Georgie Tolsen, feet up, head down in that bush and scrambling to get out. Georgie was always the one to jump out the window. Remember the boy who was always in trouble? This was the same, and here he was, out the window again—but not by design, by accident. All the children were hanging out the window with hands outstretched to help him back in, but even Georgie had a molecule of pride, so he jumped out of the bush and took off down the back road toward home.

Yessir, there was too much going on to miss Sunday school and church. If you did, what would you talk about at school on Monday? Every time there was a chance for people in the community to get together, they did, and none of the islanders missed church if they could help it. There were two churches in Buxton: one Methodist and one Pentecostal. The Pentecostal churchgoers had speaking in tongues, but the Methodists had the characters.

Buxton only had sermons every third Sunday, because the preacher was sent from the mainland to serve Hatteras Methodist Church, Trent (Frisco) Methodist Church, and Buxton Methodist Church. This was the Sunday for Buxton to hear from the preacher. When Reverend Luther came to the village, he and his family were invited by someone in the congregation to come home with them for dinner. On the island, there was dinner, and there was supper. Lunch was something you got at school. So, with the preacher in Buxton this Sunday and the ball game at the lighthouse, Charlie and Odessa Gray invited Reverend Luther and his family to come home with them, and afterward to share in the afternoon ball game. The preacher had his own car, paid for by the collection of the three congregations, so it was not necessary to take him home afterward. He also had lots of kids—six—and someone had to think twice before inviting that many people to join the already large families of the island.

Church began when the preacher got there, so there was a little time between Sunday school and church. Some people went home, but most did not. Being able to talk among themselves was a treat, and lots of news was passed around. The children were busy outside getting their clothes dirty. The girls usually congregated in groups and giggled about whatever! The boys got into races and tag and anything else that would stir up the dirt from the sandy yard. Finally Mr. Nash grabbed the long rope, rang the bell for church, and everybody went inside.

Mr. White, a local merchant and one of Charlie's circle of friends, was the president of the men's group, and he held services until it was time to introduce the preacher and his sermon. The preacher's brood sat quietly on the front bench, hands folded so angelically, and listened intently. All the other children felt sorry for them, because they had to be so good, and sorry for them that they had to sit on the side of the church where the piano was, with Miss Myrtle and her black gums and her loud voice screaming hymns into their ear. But worse was Miss Grace, who was always on the second row trying to outsing Miss Myrtle. How did they stand it?

The best part of the service was the singing. The choir was just as off-key as Miss Myrtle and her nemesis, Miss Grace, so the children felt the go-ahead to belt out the songs as much as anyone. The grown-ups mistook all that hollering to be getting in the spiritual feeling, but it was exactly the opposite. It was getting into mischief, legally!

After church, everybody got in their jalopies or trucks and headed home—some to cook for the spread at the ball game, some to feed the preacher and his gang, and some to just have a day of rest. Sunday was a day that Grandmom would not tolerate any "hammering or shooting air rifles or sawing or boisterous noise" around the land, and all the island's congregations for the most part took that seriously. It truly was the Lord's day, a day of rest, and not much work was going on. Most people even outlawed fishing on that day, and the biggest sin of all was card playing. The island almost fell silent—that is, until the ball game.

Odessa put out a spread for the preacher, and boy, did he eat. So did the rest of them. Maybe the churches didn't pay them enough, and that's why they only stayed here until they could get moved to some other town. It was not the best assignment, and only the poorest preacher would accept it. Reverend Luther was glad to get it. He had a lot of mouths to feed, and anywhere else he would be the one feeding them. Of course,

Nett and the boys were there. Bill was still on duty for Captain Charlie, and the six Luther children, Blake, Luke, and Ellie were on the porch at the kids' table.

Here was where the Luther children showed their true colors. Mary Elizabeth couldn't take her eyes off Luke, and Luke couldn't get far enough away. With all the snickering and punching from Blake, he was miserable. Ellie tried to keep Mary Elizabeth's attention away from Luke, but being younger, the older girl just brushed her off. Mike, the oldest boy, was for all the world a mean kid. He messed with his food, tried to start a food fight with his younger brother Freddy by tossing peas at him, and would have if it wasn't for Reverend Luther saying loud enough for the children to hear on the porch, "Mary Lizbeth, would you pa-ahass the pee-ahsse, plee-ahsse?" in that long, drawn-out Georgia accent he had that made the youngsters snicker during the sermon. Mary Elizabeth took the bowl from the children's table and passed it through the window from the porch to the dining room. All day long at the ballgame, Blake or Luke would walk up to Ellie and say, "Pa-ahass the pee-ahsse, plee-ahsse?" This was going to be a standing joke for absolute ever!

Grandmom's chocolate cake was more than well received, and not a crumb was left. *Guess no dessert snack tonight*, the children thought. To tell the truth, after all those people finished, there was precious little left of anything. Even the dreaded pone bread was gone, no thanks to Ellie.

The special ball game before the holiday season was at the field near the lighthouse and was between the villages of Buxton and Hatteras, the biggest rivalry. These activities taking place so close to the Coast Guard station were just as much fun for the seamen as the islanders. They never missed a game, and during the season they were part of the mix of teams playing. Although Buxton and Hatteras were the main rivals, every team wanted to beat the Coast Guard team, just for bragging rights. The Coast Guard boys had already set up long portable tables made from planks of wood on saw horses, ready for the women to cover them with tablecloths and food. There were two small homemade bleachers like stairs, also constructed by the Coast Guard, that could seat maybe thirty people. But most folks brought their own seats. One lady even had her husband put the rocking chair in the back of their truck. The rest of the people watched from blankets on the ground, or sitting in the back of someone's truck, or standing in a high stakebed truck owned by a neighbor or friend.

There was a lot going on besides the ballgame. The children were not allowed to run up and down the lighthouse steps to the tower. But they felt free to play all around the eight cement accents circling the base. Here was where all the teenagers were—each in their little groups, or a boyfriend-girlfriend situation, or around back where nobody could see what was going on. But around back in the bushes was where the more mischievous boys spied on whatever was taking place. Of course, that was where Georgie and his gang would be, barefoot and ragged from walking all the way from Buxton and Trent. The kids on the island did not consider walking as an inconvenience. They went everywhere. There were so few cars that it was understood they would walk, and it was fine. Lots of the boys had baseball gloves and played catch. Some were playing horseshoes, some boys had a circle drawn and were competing with marbles, and some just took a walk on the beach, since early November was still beautiful on Hatteras Island. The Gulf Stream ran so close to the island that it kept the ground and air warm past Thanksgiving, almost to Christmas. There was no danger in children going into the ocean while their parents watched the game. Even though the water kept the chill off the island, it was really much too cold to go swimming.

The girls had their activities also. The older girls were getting to know the Coast Guard boys, and some were playing hopscotch with a pattern drawn in the sand. Some jumped rope on the lawn near the lighthouse. Jumping rope was fun, with the more skilled girls doing double Dutch, which has two ropes crisscrossing the lines and was quite difficult. Mary Elizabeth was following poor Ellie around, questioning her about as many personal things regarding Luke as she could think of. She even asked to go see his room. Boy, did Ellie turn that one down! Blake and his friend Thomas were busy challenging all the boys near their age to a foot race. Luke was perfecting his catching with Colby.

The food was plentiful and quite a treat for the Coast Guard boys. They didn't get home cooking very much. Baskets and baskets of fried chicken, plenty of drumsticks, cornbread, more cakes and pies than anyone could eat, cookies of all sorts, various recipes for potato salad—there was also a little rivalry here—and buckets of tea with the stack of Dixie cups nearby for drinking tea or filling with potato salad. There were also long strips of wooden ice cream spoons for use as utensils. The spread also included anything someone could think of that didn't need a plate. The main dish was always fried chicken, and the various cooks with their personal recipes kept everybody eating until they were too full for anything else.

This was a ball game with bragging rights at stake—for both the game and the food. If a merchant had a grocery store and he took the trouble to bring cases of bottled drinks and tubs of water with a block of ice to keep them cool, everyone was happy to pay the dime for that.

It would seem that the game was secondary to the picnic, but that was not the case. The game was lively, and plenty of boys were around to chase down a foul ball or a home run. Most of the home runs were hit by Maurice "Dick" Burrus, a boy from Hatteras. He had gone off island for prep school and was picked up by scouts there. He was so good, he was drafted to the Boston Braves National League baseball organization. After his days of professional baseball, he came home to dominate the community league. Buxton boys always liked to play when Dick Burrus was playing. Sometimes they even won, but on this day, Hatteras won. There were other great baseball players, and they were fun to watch. Because of the Burrus boy, Hatteras usually won their games. But baseball was a great pastime for island boys, and had there been scouts to catch island games, there might have been more locals signed. These guys played barefoot, and they were good. Tommy Gray, Captain Charlie's son, was a fantastic pitcher. That was what Luke wanted to be: a pitcher like his uncle Tommy.

When the game ended, everyone helped the seamen collect their wood and take it back to the station. Others put all the trash they could find in their trucks, women got their plates hoping they were empty, and Captain Charlie and Miss Odessa had their yard back again. One thing about those games was that everybody went home with as much trash as they had brought. There was never any cleanup, as it was done by those in attendance.

At one point during the day, Luke took the Luther children to see the turtles. He kept Mike from throwing sticks at them and promised himself that he would object if the preacher and his kids came again—at least not until they had a new preacher.

That night, when putting Ellie to bed, Grandmom could tell something was bothering her. "What is it, child? This has been such a busy weekend, I have hardly had time to talk to you. Is there something you wanted to tell me?"

Ellie sighed. "Grandmom, something happened to me and Luke and Blake, and we don't know what to think about it." And with that, Ellie told her grandmother about the adventure in the woods with the Croatoan.

Grandmom listened intently, stroking Ellie's hair and encouraging her to spill all that she needed to get out. When Ellie finished, Odessa gave her a warm hug and snuggled in the bed beside her.

She began, "Sweetheart, you know your pop and I have always told you that you are special, and what you experienced was a dream. We are dreamers, you and I. We are actually dream travelers. I think I met Weroansqua when I was about Luke's age, and I talked to my mom about it. We are dreamers, that is the best I can say, and we dream about things we might have seen as having been born into a family that is protected by a special blood. Annie began to have those dreams also, but your aunt Nett never did, and neither did your aunt Iva. Because Annie stopped having them, I figured it was over, but now I realize that she stopped in order for you to pick it up, and though Aunt Nett never did, for the first time the boys got the spirit.

"These are spirit dreams, but they seem so real. They are truly a look back at your ancestors and how they lived and thought. There might be more, and if there are, you children can come to me. After all, it really is my fault that you are afflicted with this gift, and no mistaking about it, it is a gift. I don't know that anyone else on the island has it, but they could. Just nobody talks about it. And neither should you. You never can tell when it will come to be a pleasure to you or a help to someone else. It is okay to be different. Being different is probably the best gift anyone can be given. It doesn't have to be this one, but different is also considered 'special,' and as you grow older, you will appreciate being special. Now, it might go away and you will never experience it again, but with you, I don't think so. Yours is a mighty power. Can you hear other people's minds?"

"Yes," Ellie said quietly. "Mostly Luke and Blake, but Weroansqua said animals, too."

"Can you communicate with animals?" Grandmom knew the answer but wanted Ellie to get it all out.

She answered, "Yes," with the same quiet voice. "Grandmom, remember the other night when I slept late for school and had to hurry? Well, I had been in the woods with the wolves. And I could understand the deer and squirrels, too."

"Well, sweetie pie, I don't want you to be scared. All of this comes from kindness. The wolves will not hurt you, ever. Neither will the animals or the creatures of the deep. We are not the same as everyone else, and we must be thankful and careful of our gifts and use them only when needed. They are not a game to be played with, or they will be taken away.

Use them when you need them, and only for good. Now, do you want to tell the boys, or should I?"

"I will, Grandmom. Then if they want to know more, we will talk to you, but I think they will want to hear it from you, especially Blake. He is so young to have such big things happen. It is because he has me and Luke that he doesn't question things, but if he had you, too, I know he would feel better."

"All right, honey. I'm here, and what I know I will tell you, but I'll just bet you will learn more by listening to your dreams. They come from the experts. Now, go to sleep. School tomorrow, and I don't want you to be tired. Is everything okay now?"

"Yes, Grandmom. And, Grandmom, I never had a mother, but when I think about it, or somebody says something about it, I think of you, and it makes me smile inside, because I think I have two mothers—the one in heaven and you—and I feel lucky." Ellie gave her grandmom a kiss and a hug, and as Odessa stood up to fix her covers, she was already asleep.

★ 15 ★

Tom Sawyer

It was raining hard as the children got ready to go to school. Grandpop pulled the car around, and he and Ellie picked up Nett and the boys. He had to maneuver around the deep spots of the two-track road that had gullied out with water. Sometimes two of the car's wheels were up against the side portion of the road, with the other side's wheels in the water. If he had not done that, the whole car would have sunk down in the watery mud. The children liked this action, as they leaned this way or that, pretending they were on a ship. The wipers were going strong, and Nett had her feet up to keep the water off of her as it splashed up through the holes in the floorboard.

"Government needs to get us another car, don't cha think, boys?" Grandpop said. "We keep the ships straight. They ought to keep us straight."

That kept the conversation going on cars, and who had what on the island. It was true they hadn't had a car in a long time, and people had much more modern ones now. So the boys put in their choice of whose car they knew of would be a good one to ask for.

"Asking is not getting," Grandpop reminded. "Don't daydream so much." At that, all three snapped a look at the other, and the elbowing and punching started. "Calm down back there. We don't have one yet," he said, not realizing it was the "dream" comment that got them going.

"But, Grandpop, do you think they would?" All of a sudden the prospect of a new car took away all the thoughts of anything else.

"Maybe. I'll have to put in for one, and we'll see." Grandpop smiled as he already had requested a new vehicle, and he was pretty sure it was going to go through. He had not asked for anything extra ever, and this car was about to be one big hole surrounded by some metal. But as slow as the government was, there was no telling when they would get back to him. He smiled at the thought of taking these three to Manteo to pick out a car. They didn't get off the island very often, and the few times they did, it was fun for everyone.

What they liked most was being able to "ride the wash," which meant that Pop would check on the tides with the Coast Guard, and whenever low tide was, closest to daybreak, they would let some air out of the tires and drive the car over to the beach. When the tide was out, it left the banks hard and drying out—not so dry as to allow the sand to become soft, or so wet it was mud, but somewhere in between, leaving it firm, hard sand, similar to a highway. They rode the wash and laughed all the way, as the car went over what they called camelbacks, the slight hills that regularly formed when the ocean receded. It was up and down, up and down, each time bouncing them around.

Before Chicamacomico, Pop scouted for the right spot, crossing over to the dirt track running through the village, leaving the sections on the beach all around the three villages that looked okay but were actually gravel pits of broken shells, deep enough to sink a vehicle up to the running boards. These places were referred to by the locals as "red sand."

Most of the time, villagers checked around to find out who needed to go to the mainland and made a plan to caravan up together. Just in case somebody got stuck, there would be enough men to "dig 'er out." Just past Rodanthe were the flats, and two huge hills where the navy had placed metal airplane runway strips on the tracks up and over to both protect the dune and to keep cars from getting stuck going up, which made it almost impossible to push out.

Also all along the road were leftover planks in places where others had become stuck and used boards under the wheels to get traction for getting out. When that happened, they left the boards for others to use when they reached that same treacherous spot and were in the same predicament. At the flats, it was "Here we go!" and the cars pulled alongside each other and raced to the other hill. After all, the ferry could only take so many cars, and getting there late meant the end of the line, which could be long, meaning a wait for the barge to go and come back again. Also, by the time people hit the flats, they were ready for some fun after being worn out from digging each other out from the sand—or pushing free their fellow travelers from being stuck—and just going slow in general. Traveling up the beach to the ferry at Oregon Inlet was an adventure in itself. So was the ferry ride, but that is another story.

Nett asked Luke, "Son, I forgot to ask in all the commotion. Did you get your script on Friday for the play?"

"Yes, ma'am."

"What did you think?" She had turned around to see his face. If he didn't want to do it, she did not want him to have to. It wasn't easy to get in front of several communities and perform. Even with all the respect he got from the other two, he was really a shy boy who just couldn't help excelling because he worked so hard, and both he and Blake were naturally smart. Nett taught a lot of kids, and she knew the smart ones from the ones who struggled, and her boys and Ellie were some of the brightest.

"It's okay, Mom. Colby's in it, too, and Blake and Ellie. It will be fun. I know I can do it."

"Thomas is in it, too," chimed in Blake.

"But the whole play is about your character, Tom, so a lot is depending on you."

"Miss Ormond said I'd be good, and she is putting it on, and she said she would help me if I needed it, so I would like to try." Luke always took everything in stride, and he could see Blake's face. Blake was hoping he would say yes.

"Pop, we'll all be staying late today. They have their first practice. It's the play *Tom Sawyer*, and Luke is Tom, Blake and Ellie are Aunt Polly's children, and Aunt Polly is the one who took Tom in, so he lives with those three. Ormond is trying to get it ready to put it on before Thanksgiving."

"Sounds like it's a play all about us," Grandpop quipped.

"Heavens, no. Yes, there is a lot riding on Luke as Tom, but it is more about Tom and his buddies, with Sid having only a small part and Mary hardly a part at all. Actually I was hoping that Ellie would have a bigger part, but the better ones belong to the girls who fashion Tom as a boyfriend, and it certainly wouldn't do to have Ellie play one of those parts." Nett laughed.

"I don't mind not having a big part. I'm excited to get to do it at all. Most of the girls just have 'crowd' parts, and most of us don't speak anyway, so it will be fun just to be able to go to practices and watch everybody," Ellie said.

"Okay, boys, put your hats on and run. Maybe take off your shoes and socks so they don't get wet. Nett, did you bring your bumbershoot?" He used the old name for an umbrella that they used to joke about when she was sent to Raleigh for high school and came home with one. After that, she had to buy them for everybody, but she couldn't get the kids to cooperate. Rain running was more their style.

Everybody scrambled out of the car as it stopped under the trees at the top of the hill near the schoolhouse. From there, it was a dash to the closest door to beat the rain. Blake won.

School was a regular day. It was easier to study when it rained. There wasn't anything else to think about. There wouldn't be any softball today, and no sliding down the hill on boards over the pine straw, no chinaberry wars, no pine cone wars, no swinging—just school.

After the school bell rang at the end of the day, those who were taking part in the play went to the middle of the building to the auditorium. Rehearsal had been announced in the morning, as the whole school got together by grades every Monday morning for assembly. Nett played the piano while one of the high school boys, Ward, sang. Then everyone else sang some familiar songs. Ellie's favorite was "Little Sir Echo," which had a chorus of "Hello, hello, hello" sung in round-robin style by the three sections of the rows of seats. It was awhile—not until she got older— before Ellie understood the real title. She thought for a while it was "Little Sirrecco," and she didn't even get the echo part, so she missed the whole premise of the echo coming from each of the assembly sections.

The auditorium stage was large, and when it was not being used the curtain was down, and all that was seen was a huge seascape scene. The curtain was made of sailcloth and painted by a local artist. The bottom was a huge round pole given to the school by the telephone company, which had poles installed all down the beach with wire strung to connect the lines that went to the phones on the island. There were still not many phones in the villages. Most private homes did not have one, and the community generally used pay phones in the stores. The heavy pole was attached to the bottom of the sailcloth, and on either side were pulleys that, when pulled, rolled the sailcloth around the pole as it went up to reveal the stage. It was "curtain up" or "curtain down." The players got used to the shout of "Curtain," which would indicate a scene change.

The whole community used the auditorium, and most of the time the empty stage was used to store the audience seats, leaving a huge vacant room with a piano for village use. Activities were often scheduled around holidays, and for cake walks, square dancing, collective dinners, or anything that required a large hall.

Today Miss Ormond was instructing the children about their parts. This was a play put on by the school. The characters of the older people in the play—like Aunt Polly, Injun Joe, Judge Thatcher, Doc Robinson, and

Muff Potter—were played by the high school students. Other parts were Tom (Luke); Becky Thatcher, Tom's old girlfriend (Allison Quidley); the new girl, Amy, Tom's new girlfriend (Shirley Scarborough); Huck Finn (Colby); Sid (Blake); Sid's buddy (Thomas); Joe Harper (Jack Peele); and Mary (Ellie), who had only one line, with other boys and girls making up the friends and crowd. As director, Miss Ormond made sure they all got their scripts and knew the rehearsal times, and also by when each page needed to be perfected. Practice was every afternoon, with buses coming back to take students to Trent and Hatteras, Kinnakeet and Chicamacomico. Parents of the Buxton children were contacted to pick up those in the play, and most parents worked out a schedule for carpooling to allow the children to stay later.

Nett was given the music for the piano. Her task was to play dramatic music at times, happy music at times, and suspenseful music when required. This was easy for Nett, because she was the one who played the piano for the silent movies in Austin's Movie House in Hatteras. That's kind of how she met Bill, because he was so impressed by the pretty girl at the piano.

Local men—Mr. Elmer, Mr. Johnny, and others—volunteered to make the sets. Carpenters on the island always volunteered for the school's needs. Everything was decided. All they had to do was start, and that happened the next day. They planned to put it on the week before Thanksgiving. During the week before a holiday, very little schoolwork was done anyway, so they might as well make good use of the time. There was also a narrator, Mr. White. He had a rich, booming voice, and they thought he would sound just like Mark Twain. It also called for a guitar, harmonica, and percussion, all provided by high school kids. What they did not know, they would practice.

Another thing that made Hatteras special was that the island had plenty of musicians. Long winter afternoons and nights called for learning an instrument to entertain family and friends.

Bill volunteered to do the lighting. Since the villages did not have collective electricity, he worked with the 32-volt generator sent by the state to give the school electricity so that it could be used at night. The staging was a series of levels and platforms constructed of rough-hewn planks suggesting a river wharf. The setting was the Mississippi River. Each piece of the set served to depict several things. For example, the cave was an opening just left of center, and it also was used as the graveyard, for entrances and exits, and as a street before it became the mouth of the cave. Everything had multiple uses, and the skilled carpenters were anxious to make it look as real as if it had been done on Broadway in New York.

The women at the meeting were known to be masterful seamstresses, and they volunteered to make all the costumes, plus fit them to the players. It was really a community effort, and so with this many villagers involved, one wondered who would be in the audience to see the production. Answer to that: Everyone! The men bragged about their sets, the women their clothes. It was a play for everybody to get excited about. These once-a-year productions were talked about for months afterward, and sometimes as grown-ups, people even remembered what part they played when they were chosen for the school production.

The story was about a ne'er-do-well boy from Missouri who had been taken in by his aunt Polly to grow up with her and her two children, Sid and Mary. Tom was probably the Missouri counterpart to the island's Georgie Tolsen, but it would have been an insult to give the part to Georgie. Besides, who knew if he would show up, and it certainly wouldn't be every day. In the play, Tom is given chores that he is always trying to avoid. His big thing is hanging out with another boy, Huck Finn, who has only a drunken father and is sort of homeless and on the street. But his street smarts catch the admiration of Tom, who wants to be just like Huck, with nobody telling him what to do, never having to go to school, and certainly never having to do chores.

In the story, the two youngsters in the house are always telling on Tom's mischief and trying to get him in more trouble than he gets into by himself. The first scene finds Sid telling on Tom for eating jam when he isn't supposed to. Aunt Polly punishes Tom by making him whitewash the front fence next to the street. Never one to like to work, Tom uses his wits to trick the passersby into doing it for him by making believe it is fun. The whitewash scene reveals the jealousy between Becky Thatcher, daughter of the judge, and Amy, the new girl in town, both of whom are competing for Tom's attention. In another act, Tom and Becky get lost in a cave, initiating a search party, and in the last act, Tom and Huck witness a murder, which leads to a trial. Mr. White, as Mark Twain, fills in with narration the parts of the book that cannot be written into the play, thus moving the story along.

Rehearsals proved to be so much fun that lots of kids would stay late to watch, create mischief, and catch the late bus home.

The school day went on as usual, with recess and books, in that order, and even up to the day of the play, there were spirited softball games during recess. On the day before the production, Jack Peele, who played the character Joe Harper, got hit in the face with a flying bat and his lips swelled so big that they thought he wouldn't be able to deliver his line. Jack went home crying so hard about being replaced that his parents went to see Miss Ormond to beg her to let him continue. They assured her that his swelling would be down, and everything would be okay. Miss Ormond reversed her decision, because really he had not missed a single rehearsal, and she knew what it must mean to him.

The performance was set for the Tuesday before Thanksgiving holiday vacation. On that night, the auditorium began to fill up early. Everybody wanted a seat, because latecomers would have to stand in the aisles. The first/second/third-grade room was a dressing room for the boys, the fourth/fifth/sixth-grade room was a dressing room for the girls, and the seventh- and eighth-grade room was for the director and those who were waiting in line ready for their cue to go on stage. There was a lot of activity—with so much noise among the players that Mr. Austin, the principal, had to relinquish his seat in the audience and come back and quiet everyone down.

There were so many attendees that the portable shades that separated the math and science rooms on the high school side from the back of the auditorium were raised in order to provide more space for people to sit and watch.

THE PLAY:

Curtain up! Tom is getting punished by Aunt Polly for eating jam, and Sid is standing around looking smug and proud of himself for telling. Sid follows Tom over to the picket fence built by Mr. Johnny. Tom begins stopping the boys who wander down the street by singing and dancing while he pretends to whitewash the fence. He finds some takers (suckers) and exacts a prize from each as payment for being allowed to paint the fence. Huck Finn walks toward Tom swinging a dead rat (somebody's stuffed kitten toy) and repeating a rhyme:

> Barley-corn, barley corn, injun-meal shorts,
> Spunk-water, sound-water, swiller these warts.

Tom inquires as to what that means, and Huck, a bigger rascal than Tom, tells him it is a sure cure for warts. So Tom, who has several warts, asks Huck for the rat and begins the chant.

"No, no, no! That ain't it!" hollers Huck. "Then you walk away quick, seven steps, with your eyes shut, and turn around three times, and all your warts is gone!"

As Tom is getting ready to try again, Joe Harper comes on stage, and Tom sees an opportunity to get him to do the fence so that he can go off with Huck. He tells Joe how much fun it is. Huck agrees, and Tom tells Joe he will let him do it for a nickel. Joe is excited. He reaches in his pocket for the nickel and gives it to Tom, who starts to walk away with Huck, as Sid and Mary, watching, begin to go tattle to Aunt Polly that Tom is leaving. As he is walking away, Joe does his one line:

"What fart, Tom?"

Luke and Colby turn around and don't know what to say. Colby is cracking up and trying to hold it back because he is still on stage. Jack thinks maybe he didn't say his line loud enough, so again he says, "What fart, Tom?" and at that Luke and Colby literally hold each other up laughing, and poor Jack doesn't know what he's done wrong.

Again he says, "What fart, Tom?"

Blake yelled out from the other side, "Jack, you said 'Fart!'" and he rolled over on the stage laughing. By this time everyone in the audience was muffling a snort laugh, and the place was going crazy. Blake said, "Jack, you were supposed to say 'Part!' and you said 'Fart!'" and at that Blake yelled it out so loudly that bedlam broke loose everywhere.

"That's what I said!" Jack yelled out, not knowing why everyone was laughing.

Guess that bat swelled up his lips so much that he couldn't get his lips around a "P" and it came out an "F"! Needless to say, *Tom Sawyer* was the talk around every Thanksgiving table. Even though Miss Ormond yelled, "Curtain!" and Mr. White did his best Mark Twain dialog to cover all the mistakes, it never really got better than that. When the curtain went back up, everybody had regained their composure, and everything else went on without a hitch. But Jack Peele never got over the teasing about his swollen lips, and finally he started feeling pretty bold at having said such a word in front of everybody and gotten away with it. The whole school signed up for the next play, no matter what it would be. Miss Ormond and the rest of the grown-ups feared that another play any time soon would just be a disaster, with every kid trying to outdo Jack, so they switched to some other kind of entertainment—a talent show—for a while to let everybody forget about this one.

———

Thanksgiving holiday was fun. Grandmom and Nett decided they should have their family dinner with all the Gray clan at the assistant's quarters because it was twice the size of the keeper's quarters, and even Iva and Rufus were coming with their children. Still there was no second assistant hired, so they had the double lodge to themselves. Winnie, Tommy's wife, and Pete, Curt's wife, came over in the morning with their own special tasty dishes and casseroles. Along with the family, as many Coast Guard boys as wanted were invited to join them for a family dinner with Captain Charlie and Miss Odessa hosting the Thanksgiving feast. The Coast Guard boys removed the boxing ring in exchange for dinner, they were so happy to be included, and the kids were finally allowed to go up the lighthouse steps and spend some time looking at the ocean from the railing.

"If I see one of you stand up near that railing, it is going to be *you* and *me*," Grandpop warned. They were hearing that from behind them as they raced to the door of the tower.

At the top of the lighthouse, the kids sat up against the beacon and stared out at the wonderful ocean they called their playground. They talked about the adventure with the Indians and all that they remembered. They told each other about the parts of the escapade that each experienced when the others were not around. They wondered aloud if they could ever find Old Buxton again, and should they try? Ellie explained that Grandmom said they were "dream travelers," and that she wanted them to come to her if they had questions. Ellie told them both what Grandmom had said: that she had experienced dreams when she was young, but they had stopped, and even then, her dreams were not quite so detailed.

Grandmom thought the children had more of the powers than family members had ever before displayed. She was understanding about that, and she welcomed any questions they might have. But, Ellie said, Grandmom said she thought the dreams probably would not stop, and most of their questions were going to be answered in the dreams. Ellie also explained that Grandmom said they should use their own interior thoughts to ask the questions they needed answers to. She said that they might be surprised how much information they already had inside. All they had to do was ask.

This discussion lasted most of the morning, with the two older children answering all of Blake's questions and assuring him that it was the three of them all together, and they would always protect each other.

As they were talking, Luke spied a herd of right whales slowly making their way south. There were large ones and small ones. The kids became so excited that they raced down the 268 steps to strike out across the beach to sit on the sand and watch. They all wanted to be near the gigantic creatures. Luke challenged Ellie to try and use her ability to communicate with animals to just say "Hello" to the herd. Ellie concentrated, and both Luke and Blake were quiet and concentrating also. Maybe the whales heard, maybe they did not, but as each went by, they blew water out of their blow holes. What the watchers didn't know was just how close they were to meeting these giants of the deep.

EPILOGUE

It is unusual to be born and raised on such a special island. Cape Hatteras is steeped in history and has played an important part in the advancement of the United States. This is the island where the supposedly "Lost Colony" settled.

Reginald Aubrey Fessenden in 1902 sent the first musical notes from a small wireless station antenna in Buxton, one of the seven villages that make up the island. Later he achieved two-way voice transmission by radio across the Atlantic. He also produced the first sonic depth finder (fathometer) or elementary sonar. Fessenden was in competition with Guglielmo Marconi, who visited the island in 1904 to inspect property for the construction of a tower for his own experiments with wireless transmission. The better funded of the two, Marconi has often been credited with completing accomplishments that Fessenden began. The atmosphere near the island, rich in energy, being so close to the Gulf Stream, was a good conductor of electric charges, and as Fessenden had already discovered, was a great conductor of sound. Marconi built the Marconi Wireless Telegraph Company Tower near Frisco (formerly Trent), and began experimenting with the transmission of sound across the water. This tower was the first in Marconi's network.

The famous ironclad ship, the USS *Monitor*, sank in a storm off Hatteras Island.

Billy Mitchell, a frequent visitor to the island for duck hunting, chose these shores to prove that air power could sink a ship. The small airstrip here was named after him.

The first SOS distress signal from the RMS *Titanic* was received by Richard Dailey, the grandson of a winner of the Congressional Medal of Honor for Lifesaving on the Outer Banks. Richard was the wireless operator on Hatteras Island. He relayed the message to New York to a man named David Sarnoff (founder of RCA), who reprimanded Dailey for "junking up the airwaves" with what Sarnoff considered a hoax. Had they paid attention some of the passengers might have been saved.

The tallest brick lighthouse in the world, located in Buxton, has drawn millions of visitors over the years. Moving this structure away from the ocean in 1999 was called the "Move of the Century." More than one thousand ships are buried off the coast at Diamond Shoals, referred to as the "graveyard of the Atlantic." Aaron Burr's daughter, Theodosia Burr, being one of those lost at sea, was considered one of the many victims. The famous surfmen of Rodanthe, another village, saved dozens of ships and crews. Many received the Congressional Medal of Honor for Lifesaving.

Legendary pirates like Blackbeard walked the island and sold booty to the citizens. These and many more interesting facts will be presented in this series, *The Lighthouse Kids: Spirits of Cape Hatteras Island*. The five books in the series are: *Croatoan, Legends and Lore, Pirates, Surfmen and Shipwrecks*, and *Under Attack*.

The books were written for young readers as well as curious adults, who will also marvel at the facts they uncover. The volumes tell the history of the island; the down-home style of the natives (as they were not connected to the mainland before 1950); the legends that have grown up around the Indians, pirates, and wrecks; and the German submarine attacks in World War II. Readers are introduced to the occupants of the Atlantic Ocean. They are our neighbors, and their existence proved most important to islanders. The stories are laced with the morality and strength passed on from generations—humorous stories witnessed or heard by my mother, who lived to age 102, and told at her father's knee. Many of the elder islanders remember what it was like when we were the only ones here—long before the bridge, highway, Park Service, and tourists.

The situations are real as I have experienced them. There is mystery, magic, history, and adventure. The facts are *true*; you are invited to check. It is a different kind of history book.

Many characters' names are fictitious. The family names are true. The only names used exactly as they are registered are those whose accomplishments and exploits have been recorded as history. Their dialogue can only be imagined, but their actions are documented as fact.

Odessa Scarborough Jennette Gray had three brothers who were lighthouse keepers: Unaka B. Jennette, Cape Hatteras Lighthouse in Buxton, North Carolina, on the island of Cape Hatteras; Utah C. Jennette, Cape Henry Lighthouse in Virginia Beach, Virginia; and Alaska D. Jennette, Rock Point Lighthouse in Rock Point, Maryland. There, Alaska first met General Billy Mitchell and persuaded him to pursue wildfowl hunting on Cape Hatteras Island. The second book in the series chronicles those visits and his later accomplishments on this island.

The Jennette family donated four acres of land on which to build the first lighthouse, in 1802, and the U.S. government paid $12.50 for each acre. The family had eight of the Cape Hatteras Lighthouse keepers over the following years.

Odessa's husband, Charles Poole Gray, was a graduate of North Carolina State University, formerly the North Carolina College of Agriculture and Mechanic Arts, where he was a member of the Kappa Alpha fraternity. He served as principal of the consolidated schools of Cape Hatteras for forty-three years and was in the hierarchy of the Masonic Lodge. He served as the first county commissioner for Cape Hatteras Island in Dare County. The Cape Hatteras High School library is dedicated to him. He owned one of the largest general stores in the village of Buxton and kept the accounts of countless members of the community, which he willingly destroyed during the Great Depression, never collecting from the people who could not pay.

He was a builder as well as a teacher. Captain Charlie in this book is fashioned after "Mr. Charlie." The mannerisms and temperament are indicative of his style. He did bring electric lights to the island and still has numerous papers in the Library of Congress.

Grandmom Dessa could trace her ancestry back to the Croatoan Indian times on Hatteras Island.

Baxter B. Miller was married to Charlie Gray's sister Josephine and could trace his family back nine generations on the island. He was awarded U.S. Lifesaving medals in both gold and silver. His son Lindwood, "Lindy," was the teen who found the antique sword described in the book. The family turned it over to the Historical Society of North Carolina.

The Croatoan history is real. Weroansqua was the mother of the great Manteo, and they lived on Cape Hatteras Island. The fact that Manteo rescued the remaining members of the first Roanoke colony is well documented. All Indian names are true.

Island life is depicted as it was: the schools, the churches, the life and fun times are real places and events. The children's names have been changed. The hurricanes are described as they happened and were experienced.

To be released shortly, the second book in the *Lighthouse Kids* series, *Legends and Lore*, retells the stories passed down from the elders through the years. Many legends are retold in the continuous saga of this tiny strip of sand. The people who found fame from their exploits are featured, as well as the look of the island in those early times before we were connected to the mainland. Those of us who were lucky enough to have roots here and have experienced the style of living that was perpetuated from our ancestors have a legacy to pass on to others.

In *Legends and Lore* are descriptions of the ocean around us—what lives there, how they live, and how the islanders lived with them. The fictional history of the Jennette women is told in relation to the island's history.

We have tales to tell and would like for those who have chosen to associate with this part of the earth to share in the way this island grew into modern society. We were totally isolated from outside civilization for a long time, but we were never alone. The world decided long ago to come to us, and we accepted what it delivered. We might have reshaped it a little, but we kept up, as you will see in the upcoming *Legends and Lore*. Sometimes it's not what you would expect, but it was redone "Hatteras style."

Welcome to one of the edges of the world. We are as far east as one can go and still claim to be in the United States.

AFTERWORD: CROATOAN

"Croatoan" was the last word spoken by Edgar Allan Poe.

"Croatoan" is written in the journal of Amelia Earhart in 1937.

"Croatoan" was carved into the bedpost of Ambrose Bierce while in Mexico in 1913.

"Croatoan" was scratched on the wall of a cell that stagecoach robber Black Bart inhabited before he was released from prison in 1888, never to be seen again.

"Croatoan" was written on the last page of the logbook of the ghost ship *Carroll A. Deering*, which ran aground on Diamond Shoals in 1921.

ACKNOWLEDGMENTS

These books are dedicated to my mother, Jeanette Gray Finnegan, who died at 102 years old before she could "hold the books in her hand." She was blind during her last years, but her friend Rita, who stayed with her at night, read every manuscript to her, almost as a bedtime story.

I also owe the entire series of books to my grandsons, Luke and Blake, whose personalities permeate the pages through the actions of the main characters.

I attribute the lion's share of thanks to my husband, Ted Torok, who anticipated every single chapter with encouragement, and reinforced my resolve to continue writing despite all the distractions and interruptions. His enthusiasm for learning the history of the island on which I planted him fueled the project.

ABOUT THE AUTHOR

Jeanette Gray Finnegan Jr. was born in what was, then, the weather bureau building, in the back room with one hospital bed, a local midwife, medicines, and multiple shortwave radios which could be used to contact the hospitals on the mainland. Her place of birth, Hatteras village, was the closest place for a plane to land should the patient need to be "taken off" (island speak for "one too sick to be attended to by anyone without a medical degree").

She spent her childhood surrounded by an extended family of grandparents, uncles, and kin.

During World War II, while her father and uncles fought in both the Atlantic and Pacific theaters she, her older brother, and her mother lived in the big room upstairs in her grandparents' house.

Jaye, as she is known, moved "off island" to attend high school and college, and taught secondary school for thirty-five years in the Virginia public school system before coming back to the island to live.

She writes in the solitude of the third floor loft of her home, with views of both sound and sea. Surrounded by books—borrowed, bought, downloaded, or checked out from various libraries—she studied the written history of the island, and wove the tales in these books from fact, experience, and a grandmother's longing to convey the island's history to her grandchildren.

The impact of growing up in this magical place, and her pride in the people of the island and their accomplishments, permeate the pages.